上海大学管理学院教育管理研究中心丛书

Summer for Thee Grant I May Be

但愿我是你的夏日

英文诗选译

金一潇 编译

上海大学出版社

图书在版编目（CIP）数据

但愿我是 你的夏日：英文诗选译／金一潇编译
.——上海：上海大学出版社，2023.7
ISBN 978-7-5671-4759-1

Ⅰ.①但… Ⅱ.①金… Ⅲ.①诗集－世界 Ⅳ.
①I12

中国国家版本馆 CIP 数据核字 (2023) 第 122266 号

责任编辑　石伟丽
技术编辑　金　鑫　　钱宇坤
装帧设计　倪天辰

书　　名	但愿我是 你的夏日：英文诗选译
编　　译	金一潇
出版发行	上海大学出版社
社　　址	上海市上大路 99 号
邮政编码	200444
网　　址	http://www.shupress.cn
发行热线	021-66135112
出 版 人	戴骏豪
印　　刷	上海东亚彩印有限公司
经　　销	各地新华书店
开　　本	710mm×1000mm
印　　张	17.5
字　　数	350 千
版　　次	2023 年 7 月第 1 版
印　　次	2023 年 7 月第 1 次
书　　号	978-7-5671-4759-1/I·690
定　　价	98.00 元

版权所有　侵权必究
如发现本书有印装质量问题请与印刷厂质量科联系
联系电话：021-34536788

序
——但愿我们是你的夏日

三年前的一个夏夜，我和一潇还有几个朋友相约在茶馆里聊天。临别的时候已经将近午夜，意犹未尽的我们缓缓走出茶馆。一潇谈到了最近正在创作的诗集，于是我们就着昏黄的路灯，站在新天地的一个十字路口，热火朝天地继续聊起了诗和一切。在万籁俱寂的深夜，他的眼睛里闪烁着光芒。我能看到这个年轻人身上对中西方文化的通晓和热爱。通过我三十多年的教学经验，从那时起我就确定这群年轻人将成为未来教育行业一束特别的光。

21世纪是一个信息高度发达、节奏非常迅猛、人心却无比不安的年代。科技的革命让我们在即时满足的快感中，忘记了给心灵的滋养留出一份静候的空间。

百年前，东西方思想文化给人的感觉像是各自为阵、彼此遥望，从语言、生活习惯到思维方式都仿佛站在了迥然不同的立场。只是多年来的探索都在试图模块化拼接组合中西各自可视化的部分。时至今日，国际化的进程需要当今社会能对东西方都有全面的认知和了解，教育不再单独被割裂成西方或者东方的派系，中西互望像一面镜子，在彼此的眼中照见彼此，中西融合的概念于是应运而生。在中西互望的过程中，我们愈发强烈地感受到中国文化屹立于世界的民族自信。

Summer for Thee　Grant I May Be

或许探究背后深层次的一致性，是我们更应尝试的地方，比如情感、生命关怀、真善美等等。求同存异是中国文化最美妙的地方，对比参照式的教学方法或许更契合当下孩子们的学习模式，能让我们站在东方的视角，同样可以去鸟瞰全球所有文明的璀璨，让我们的生命更显饱满。

根据中国科学院的一项调查，我国青少年抑郁检出率为24.6%。这是不是一个无解的问题呢？在我看来，这些问题其实是因为孩子们的生活和情感与现实产生了严重的割裂。而教育的目的不是改变，而是循序渐进地进行影响和感化。所谓"感化"并不是靠逻辑层面的道理，而是一种逐步影响的过程。很多时候，去滋养内心最好的方式就是通过美育和艺术。

诗歌是艺术的一种——通过美学的高度与愉快的感官体验，给予孩子一部分温暖和力量，从而帮助孩子真正认识、理解和成为自己。

诗句中穿越千年依然真挚的情感直到今天仍旧在打动我们。在阅读这些浓缩的永恒的情感时，这一刻我们得以直视被忽略已久的内心。

在漫漫人生中，总有那么些时刻，我们的内心会和唐诗相碰撞、相感发——浮现出"白毛浮绿水，红掌拨清波"的清丽画卷，体会出"大漠孤烟直，长河落日圆"的雄壮契阔，品味出"近乡情更怯，不敢问来人"的无奈怅然，领悟出"愿君多采撷，此物最相思"的暗流涌动。

本书所收录的诗歌背后，是诗人们百年前的内心独白、对人生的思考以及对内心情感的表达。通过赏析古人们拥有情感、认知情感、表达情感的过程，感受诗歌恰好给予的现代人生活所缺失的一部分生命力量。我们希望能够让孩子们心中留下一些简单易读、便于理解的真善美体验，通过情感的共振最终给孩子们带来一定的生命震撼。

对于低龄的孩子来说，诗歌的浸染可以培养他们拥有一颗永远温暖而炽热的内心。通过精练的诗句提升孩子对语言的美感，用美感激发孩子对文字的向往，由向往催生学习的内驱力，由内驱力产生对这个世界真正的爱。一个孩子如果内心没有温暖没有爱，将来不可能爱他人、爱事业，也很难建立起兴趣方向和远期目标。没有爱的基础，这一切都不会顺应而来。

通过阅读这些或铿锵有力、或含蓄婉约、或壮丽恢宏、或优雅空灵的诗句，孩子们将生发出柔软、坚定而丰盈的内心，使其成为在瞬息万变的世界中可以主动追求和把握的东西，帮助孩子们不在人生的风雨飘摇中失去方向，从而形成一种内在的完整性。诗歌，可以让悲观者温暖，让无力者有力，让迷失者前行。

正是出于这种富有美感的冲击，我们产生了将它们化为有声语言的冲动。于是我重拾多年前的播音工作，录下了将近上百首诗。当有一位妈妈把我录的诗歌给孩子听的时候，起初孩子的眼睛里闪烁着似懂非懂的光芒，凝神半天后孩子跟妈妈说："妈妈，我听完这首诗，感觉到内心好想哭。"虽然他的语言不足以表达他的悲伤，但是他纯真直白的话语表现出他被诗里的内容所深深打动了。

在急功近利的浮躁氛围和不计其数的突破进化中，我们的团队实现了难得可贵的"慢教育"。在教育行业能够遇到如此坚守的"逆行者"，让我感到充满力量。借着这样一个机会，我也想向身边所有这些热爱着教育、关心着未来的人们，表达发自内心的敬意。

"孩子其实是成人的榜样。"我们不断追求返璞归真的生命力，试图能够重新用纯真和简单的思维方式来看待这个世界。同样，希望这些文字能给孩子们带来更多的思考探索以及无与伦比的美感体验——但愿我们是你的夏日。

雷礼

致洪苏昕和所有孩子的秋颂

有年份的花体字　应该是　无比鲜艳
他们依偎在一起　守护　一些珍贵时间
可再怎么还原　也只是　白纸黑字的从前

那天　阳光尚未疲倦　风刚好吹过屋檐
而光影　定格在一张　与你有关的画面
一枚落叶　秋色微甜　你　稚嫩的侧脸
此刻　美好　被诠释得　太显眼

亲爱的　我只是又反复观看了　好几遍
闭上眼许愿　给这段美好　一段长长的期限
默念得很轻　很小心　只想我们彼此　能听见

金一潇

Emily
Dickinson

艾米莉·狄金森

1

William
Butler
Yeats

威廉·巴特勒·叶芝

37

William
Wordsworth

威廉·华兹华斯

61

目录

William Shakespeare
威廉·莎士比亚
165

George Gordon Byron
乔治·戈登·拜伦
91

John Keats
约翰·济慈
217

Percy Bysshe Shelley
珀西·比希·雪莱
121

Emily Dickinson

艾米莉·狄金森
1830—1886

　　美国女诗人。与华尔特·惠特曼一同被称为美国诗歌星空中的"双子星"。狄金森惊人的创作力为世人留下近 1800 首诗，但是生前只发表过 7 首，其余的都在她去世后才出版并逐渐被世人所知。

　　狄金森的父亲是一位律师，对她的学习格外用心，父亲让狄金森从小到学校接受系统的教育。父亲也非常喜欢文学，在父亲的影响下，狄金森从小喜欢阅读美国作家爱默生的书籍，并在她二十几岁的时候开始诗歌创作。

　　狄金森的诗主要写生活、自然、友情等，风格凝练婉约、清新自然。代表作有《头脑，比天空更加宽广》《我们学完了全部爱的魔法》《晨曦比以往来得更加温柔》等。

Emily Dickinson
艾米莉 · 狄金森

Summer for Thee, Grant I May Be

If Recollecting Were Forgetting

I'm Nobody! Who Are You?

Success Is Counted Sweetest

Heart ! We Will Forget Him

The Morns Are Meeker Than They Were

The Bee Is Not Afraid of Me

Will There Really Be a "Morning"?

但愿我是，你的夏日	6
如果记忆是为了忘记	8
我姓何名谁！你又是谁？	9
成功的滋味满是甜蜜	10
心灵，我们终将把他忘记	12
晨曦比以往来得更加温柔	14
蜜蜂对我完全不设防线	16
试问那里是否真有一个"早晨"？	18

Emily Dickinson
艾米莉·狄金森

If I Shouldn't Be Alive

Dreams—Are Well—but Waking's Better

This Is My Letter to the World

"Why Do I Love" You, Sir?

We Learned the Whole of Love

The Brain—Is Wider Than the Sky

A Secret Told

Summer for Thee Grant I May Be

若我那时已经离开了人间　　20

梦里美若红尘，醒来更为情深　　22

这是我写给全世界的信　　24

先生，"为何我深爱着"你？　　26

我们学完了全部爱的魔法　　30

头脑，比天空更加宽广　　32

秘密一旦说出口　　34

Summer
for Thee, Grant I May Be

Summer for thee, grant I may be
When Summer days are flown!
Thy music still, when Whippoorwill
And Oriole—are done!

For thee to bloom, I'll skip the tomb
And row my blossoms o'er!
Pray gather me—Anemone—
Thy flower—forevermore!

但愿我是，
你的夏日

但愿我是，你的夏日
时光未止，夜凉如石！
袅袅如丝，其音若至
夜莺启诗，黄鹂漫词！

花开之时，我心飞驰
花语情思，行行入痴！
纤手所指，野棉为誓——
无关生死，落花成诗！

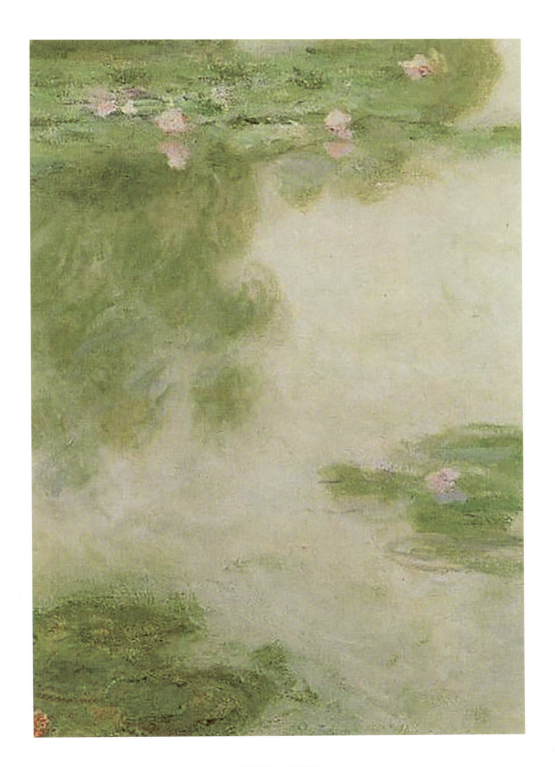

但愿我是 你的夏日

如果记忆是为了忘记

如果记忆是为了忘记,
那我此生将不再回忆。
如果忘记是为了记忆,
那我曾如此接近忘却。
如果思念是十里长笛,
如果哀泣是悦染琉璃,
那我想用轻盈的手指
采集今日里最美的你!

If recollecting were forgetting,

Then I remember not.

And if forgetting, recollecting,

How near I had forgot.

And if to miss, were merry,

And if to mourn, were gay,

How very blithe the fingers

That gathered this, Today!

If Recollecting Were Forgetting

I'm Nobody! Who are you?
Are you—Nobody—too?
Then there's a pair of us!
Don't tell! they'd advertise—you know!

How dreary—to be—Somebody!
How public—like a Frog—
To tell your name—the livelong June—
To an admiring Bog!

I'm Nobody! Who Are You?

我姓何名谁!你又是谁?

我姓何名谁!你又是谁?
难道你也是,人们眼中的无名之辈?
我们是天造地设的一对!
但你知道,他们会大肆胡吹!

为自己正名,好不无聊!
哪怕做只青蛙,也要面对沼泽的高傲——
漫长的六月对你在呼啸
何等招摇,可又有谁能知道!

但愿我是 你的夏日

Success is counted sweetest
By those who ne'er succeed.
To comprehend a nectar
Requires sorest need.

成功的滋味满是甜蜜
是追梦人此生的预期。
这琼浆玉露里的甜腻
最痛的渴望才能触及。

Success Is Counted Sweetest

Not one of all the purple host
Who took the flag today
Can tell the definition
So clear of victory.

As he, defeated—dying—
On whose forbidden ear
The distant strains of triumph
Burst agonized and clear!

成功的滋味满是甜蜜

在紫色队列的人海里
他执掌并高举着大旗
没有人能比他更熟悉
这颗胜利果实的真谛。

如果他战至奄奄一息
耳边只有哀嚎的哭泣
远处飘来凯旋的风笛
满满的是痛苦的清晰!

Heart !
We Will Forget Him

Heart! We will forget him!

You and I—tonight!

You may forget the warmth he gave—

I will forget the light!

When you have done, pray tell me

That I may straight begin!

Haste! lest while you're lagging

I remember him!

心灵，我们终将把他忘记

心灵，我们终将而且必须把他忘记！
今夜就是最佳的时机，你和我一起！
你可以忘却那些他曾经温暖的记忆——
而我要忘记他光芒曾照耀过的土地！

当你删除完毕，是否能给我个信息
这样我便会立马开始并且用尽全力！
快！你任何的一丝延误都无比危机
哪怕仅半口喘息，我都会把他想起！

The Morns Are Meeker Than They Were

The morns are meeker than they were—
The nuts are getting brown—
The berry's cheek is plumper—
The Rose is out of town—

The maple wears a gayer scarf—
The field—a scarlet gown—
Lest I sh'd seem old fashioned
I'll put a trinket on.

晨曦
比以往来得更加温柔

晨曦比以往来得更加温柔——
坚果被喷上了棕色的彩绣——
浆果的脸颊如此圆润剔透——
玫瑰的出走小镇没有挽留——

华丽的围巾是枫叶的独有——
田野把鲜红大衣披在肩头——
生怕不经意，潮流成腐朽
我拿着胸针，别在了胸口。

Summer for Thee Grant I May Be

The Bee Is Not Afraid of Me

The Bee is not afraid of me.

I know the Butterfly.

The pretty people in the Woods

Receive me cordially—

The Brooks laugh louder when I come—

The Breezes madder play;

Wherefore mine eye thy silver mists,

Wherefore, Oh Summer's Day?

蜜蜂对我完全不设防线

蜜蜂对我完全不设防线。
我也同样熟知那些蝴蝶。
林间的居民在安居乐业
而且他们待我也很亲切——

来时溪水笑得更欢了些——
清风的嬉戏也更加狂野；
为何我眼里满是你银色的摇曳，
这才发觉，又到了夏日的季节？

Will There Really Be a "Morning"?

Will there really be a "Morning"?
Is there such a thing as "Day"?
Could I see it from the mountains
If I were as tall as they?

Has it feet like Water lilies?
Has it feathers like a Bird?
Is it brought from famous countries
Of which I have never heard?

Oh some Scholar! Oh some Sailor!
Oh some Wise Man from the skies!
Please to tell a little Pilgrim
Where the place called "Morning" lies!

试问那里是否真有一个"早晨"?

试问那里是否真有一个"早晨"?
那里是否存在着"白昼的时针"?
我能否在山上发现它的真身
倘若我也像那般高大如山峰?

它是否有像睡莲那样的须根?
它是否有鸟儿般的翎羽丰润?
是否由盛名的国度落地传承
而我竟然对此完全闻所未闻?

博学的高人!老练的掌舵人!
或者那普渡人间智慧的象征!
能否告知这渺小的朝圣之人
何处是"早晨",还是南柯一梦!

If I Shouldn't Be Alive

If I shouldn't be alive

When the Robins come,

Give the one in Red Cravat,

A Memorial crumb.

If I couldn't thank you,

Being fast asleep,

You will know I'm trying

With my Granite lip!

若我那时已经
离开了人间

若我那时已经离开了人间
在知更鸟前来拜访的那天
请给红领结的那位多一点
多一点面包屑和我的思念

若我无法诉说感谢的语言
因为我永眠在虚无的空间
我相信你终将把我的努力听见
僵硬的唇间永远唱着我的爱恋

Dreams—are well—but Waking's better,

If One wake at Morn—

If One wake at Midnight—better—

Dreaming—of the Dawn—

Sweeter—the Surmising Robins—

Never gladdened Tree—

Than a Solid Dawn—confronting—

Leading to no Day—

Dreams—Are Well— but Waking's Better

梦里美若红尘，醒来更为情深，
如果梦醒时分，在微醺的早晨——
如果午夜惊魂，你也不必伤神——
这样你便能把黎明揉进你的梦——

更甜的香芬来自知更鸟的真诚——
却从未听闻树木那爽朗的笑声——
却好过不变的黎明终将更伤人——
即便比起那个永远未知的时辰——

梦里美若红尘，
醒来更为情深

这是我写给全世界的信

This Is My Letter to the World

This is my letter to the World

That never wrote to Me—

The simple News that Nature told—

With tender Majesty

Her Message is committed

To Hands I cannot see—

For love of Her—Sweet—countrymen

Judge tenderly—of Me

这是我写给全世界的信
可它却从未给过我回应——
自然诉说着简单的事情——
满是温柔又庄严的动听

她信息的投递我很确信
我放在了看不见的手心——
为了爱她,同胞们,我的至亲
评判我时,可否请,略带柔情

"Why Do I Love" You, Sir?

先生,"为何我深爱着"你?

"Why do I love" You, Sir?

Because—

The Wind does not require the Grass

To answer—Wherefore when He pass

She cannot keep Her place.

先生,"为何我深爱着"你?
因为——
凛冽的风从不会对小草追问到底
让她去回忆,为何当风吹到这里
小草便不得不离开这生根的土地。

Because He knows—and

Do not You—

And We know not—

Enough for Us

The Wisdom it be so—

The Lightning—never asked an Eye

Wherefore it shut—when He was by—

Because He knows it cannot speak—

And reasons not contained—

Of Talk—

There be—preferred by Daintier Folk—

The Sunrise—Sire—compelleth Me—

Because He's Sunrise—and I see—

Therefore—Then—

I love Thee—

因为他对此无比熟悉，和你相比
你却完全不知该从何又如何想起——
我们也无从查起，又如何去分析——
但是有时无心的一笔，便是足以
倘若有如此般的智慧深埋在心底——

炫丽的闪电从不问眼睛是否留意
为何当他划过天际，眼睛却紧闭——
因为他知道眼睛没有说话的能力——
更何况有些道理，又要从何说起——
即便能把它讲起，也会词不达意——
高雅的人们会静待它渐渐地清晰——

日出的瑰丽，先生，我情难自已——
因为他是这份亮丽，我为此着迷——
所以，往事不提，而我一不留意——
坠入时光的缝隙，一眼便爱上你——

We Learned the Whole of Love

We learned the Whole of Love—
The Alphabet—the Words—
A Chapter—then the mighty Book—
Then—Revelation closed—

But in Each Other's eyes
An Ignorance beheld—
Diviner than the Childhood's—
And each to each, a Child—

Attempted to expound
What Neither—understood—
Alas, that Wisdom is so large—
And Truth—so manifold!

我们学完了全部爱的魔法

我们学完了全部爱的魔法——
所有字母以及词汇的表达——
从一段文法接着一本词话——
直到闭合了启示录的面纱——

但是我们彼此眼眸里的画
却察觉到一种无知的尴尬——
可它远比幼稚看来更典雅——
彼此对视然后孩子般喧哗——

曾试图深挖那背后的真话
然而这些学问竟无人能答——
惊讶，智慧竟然如此博大——
而真理的模样又如此复杂！

但愿我是　你的夏日

The Brain—
Is Wider Than the Sky

The Brain—is wider than the Sky—

For—put them side by side—

The one the other will contain

With ease—and You—beside—

The Brain is deeper than the sea—

For—hold them—Blue to Blue—

The one the other will absorb—

As Sponges—Buckets—do—

The Brain is just the weight of God—

For—Heft them—Pound for Pound—

And they will differ—if they do—

As Syllable from Sound—

头脑，
比天空更加宽广

头脑，比天空更加宽广——
只要，让他们靠近对方——
一个便能把另一个挽上——
轻巧，而且与你也一样——

头脑，比海洋更会深藏——
他们一个深蓝一个忧伤——
一个能把另一个吸附上——
像海绵，也像水桶一样——

头脑与上帝有相同重量——
把他们称重一磅对一磅——
他们终将出现异常，这种异样——
好比音节绝不同于歌唱的声响——

A Secret Told

秘密一旦说出口

A Secret told—

Ceases to be a Secret—then—

A Secret—kept—

That—can appal but One—

Better of it—continual be afraid—

Than it—

And Whom you told it to—beside—

秘密一旦说出口，哪怕只半点走漏——

也就，即刻失去了秘密独有的不朽——

秘密一旦能保留，只要今生不泄露——

再愁，惊恐也只会让他一人去承受——

那么最好保留，继续在惊慌里担忧——

不然还能有怎样的理由，或是借口——

让哪一位你的挚友来分担你的忧愁——

William Butler Yeats

威廉·巴特勒·叶芝
1865—1939

爱尔兰诗人、剧作家和散文家,是爱尔兰文艺复兴运动的领袖,代表作有《当你老了》《漫步幽静的柳树园》等。

叶芝出生在具有艺术气息的家庭,他的父亲是位画家,还经常跟他一起朗读莎士比亚、司各特的诗。从小的诗歌熏陶让叶芝爱上了诗歌创作。

叶芝于1923年获得诺贝尔文学奖,他的诗被称为"鼓舞人心的诗篇"。他也被诗人艾略特称为"当代最伟大的诗人"。

William Butler Yeats
威廉·巴特勒·叶芝

When You Are Old

Down by the Salley Gardens

The Lake Isle of Innisfree

The White Birds

Into the Twilight

He Tells of the Perfect Beauty

The Arrow

O Do Not Love Too Long

A Song

A Deep-sworn Vow

Summer for Thee Grant I May Be

当你老了	40
漫步幽静的柳树园	42
茵纳斯弗利岛	44
白色的鸳鸯	46
走进暮霭	48
他永远的沉鱼落雁	50
光阴似箭，莫道从前	52
请别爱得太久	54
一首心歌	56
心的誓言	59

但愿我是　你的夏日

When You Are Old

When you are old and grey and full of sleep,

And nodding by the fire, take down this book,

And slowly read, and dream of the soft look

Your eyes had once, and of their shadows deep;

How many loved your moments of glad grace,

And loved your beauty with love false or true,

But one man loved the pilgrim Soul in you,

And loved the sorrows of your changing face;

And bending down beside the glowing bars,

Murmur, a little sadly, how Love fled

And paced upon the mountains overhead

And hid his face amid a crowd of stars.

当你老了

当你年老鬓发白,当你睡眼昏沉沉,
倚在炉边打个盹,取下了图书一本,
阅读慢慢路漫漫,回忆从这里启程
你曾有温柔眼神,眼神里眼波深深;

你也曾倾国倾城,你也曾风靡万人,
所有对你的情深,必定都真假难分,
只有我爱你是真,我爱你圣洁的心,
还有那岁月风霜,留在你脸上的吻;

蹒跚弯腰在炉灯,辗转无眠望星辰,
喃喃自语谁听闻,情到浓时又伤神
多情如残花烟冷,为爱曾勇攀高峰
爱神已悄然离去,繁星里面孔无存。

(编译者注:致敬诗人子尤、恩师江蔚东)

Down by the salley gardens my love and I did meet;
She passed the salley gardens with little snow-white feet.
She bid me take love easy, as the leaves grow on the tree;
But I, being young and foolish, with her would not agree.

In a field by the river my love and I did stand,
And on my leaning shoulder she laid her snow-white hand.
She bid me take life easy, as the grass grows on the weirs;
But I was young and foolish, and now am full of tears.

漫步幽静的柳树园
Down by the Salley Gardens

漫步幽静的柳树园,我与心爱的人就这样遇见;
她点着轻盈的脚尖,在香径上撒下了一路白雪。
她说爱情不必眷恋,就像树梢终究会挂满绿叶;
但我的天真太肤浅,就这样今生错过了你的缘。

漫步宁静的溪流边,我与心爱的人已走了好远,
她搭着我微倾的肩,这双手看起来是如此皎洁。
她说人生无须彰显,就像小草终究会铺满岸边;
曾经的天真太肤浅,恍然之间泪水模糊了视线。

Summer for Thee Grant I May Be

但愿我是 你的夏日

The Lake Isle of Innisfree

I will arise and go now, and go to Innisfree,

And a small cabin build there, of clay and wattles made;

Nine bean-rows will I have there, a hive for the honey-bee,

And live alone in the bee-loud glade.

And I shall have some peace there, for peace comes dropping slow,

Dropping from the veils of the morning to where the cricket sings;

There midnight's all a glimmer, and noon a purple glow,

And evening full of the linnet's wings.

I will arise and go now, for always night and day

I hear lake water lapping with low sounds by the shore;

While I stand on the roadway, or on the pavements grey,

I hear it in the deep heart's core.

茵纳斯弗利岛

我即将起航,前往一个名叫茵纳斯弗利的地方,
我会用藤条与泥浆,在那里筑起我专属的新房;
我将架起芸豆九行,然后为蜜蜂也列一个蜂箱,
独居的时光,我躺在绿荫下把美妙的蜂鸣独享。

我闻到了宁静的芬芳,而它在缓缓洒落我身旁,
伴着朦胧的朝阳一路坠落到蟋蟀们歌唱的故乡;
午夜里闪烁着微光,正午当空下一片紫气洋洋,
黄昏时成群的红雀舞动着翅膀为天空抹上红妆。

我又即将起航,前往那个让我魂牵梦萦的地方
每晚我都在梦里欣赏浪花与河畔那动情的合唱;
不论我在车水马龙的街上还是灯光昏黄的小巷,
悠扬的回响在心底荡漾,朝思暮想,角徵宫商。

但愿我是 你的夏日

I would that we were, my beloved, white birds on the foam of the sea!

We tire of the flame of the meteor, before it can fade and flee;

And the flame of the blue star of twilight, hung low on the rim of the sky,

Has awaked in our hearts, my beloved, a sadness that may not die.

A weariness comes from those dreamers, dew-dabbled, the lily and rose;

Ah, dream not of them, my beloved, the flame of the meteor that goes,

Or the flame of the blue star that lingers hung low in the fall of the dew:

For I would we were changed to white birds on the wandering foam: I and

I am haunted by numberless islands, and many a danaan shore,

Where Time would surely forget us, and Sorrow come near us no more;

Soon far from the rose and the lily and fret of the flames would we be,

Were we only white birds, my beloved, buoyed out on the foam of the sea!

The White Birds

白色的鸳鸯

亲爱的,但愿我们能变成那对在海浪上翱翔着的白色鸳鸯!
流星还未黯淡地逃向远方,然而我们已经厌倦了它的光芒;
看那暮色里湛蓝星的火光,在天幕之下给岁月染尽了红霜,
被唤醒的暮霭沉沉的忧伤,把美好的幻想在我们心底埋葬。

梦里依然满是疲倦的迷茫,即便水灵的百合玫瑰又能怎样;
亲爱的,千万别把它们念想,流星的闪亮转瞬便殆尽消亡,
即便天际凝露下那摇曳的湛蓝星的火光,也把它通通遗忘:
我多希望与你化为一对白色的鸳鸯,凭海飞翔,为爱合唱!

远方无数的岛屿和醉人的海岸在我的朝思暮想里缓缓流淌,
在那里时光终将把我们遗忘,忧伤也将无法靠近我们身旁;
让我们快快逃离这哀伤的玫瑰百合和远方烦闷惆怅的星光,
亲爱的试想我们是那对白色的鸳鸯,凭海飞翔,终成绝响!

Out-worn heart, in a time out-worn,

Come clear of the nets of wrong and right;

Laugh, heart, again in the grey twilight,

Sigh, heart, again in the dew of the morn.

Your mother Eire is always young,

Dew ever shining and twilight grey;

Though hope fall from you and love decay,

Burning in fires of a slanderous tongue.

Come, heart, where hill is heaped upon hill:

For there the mystical brotherhood

Of sun and moon and hollow and wood

And river and stream work out their will;

And God stands winding His lonely horn,

And time and the world are ever in flight;

And love is less kind than the grey twilight,

And hope is less dear than the dew of the morn.

Into the Twilight

Summer for Thee Grant I May Be

走进暮霭

这个残缺的心灵，在这个破败的时代，
快跳出那无形的网，网面只有黑与白；
欢笑吧心灵，昏暗的天幕又将被拉开，
叹息吧心灵，我们又即将把晨露迎来。

你的祖国母亲爱尔兰将永远青春常在，
曾经露水晶莹现在暮光也被灰暗淹埋；
尽管希望在落空并且爱情也逐渐衰败，
最终都将被流言蜚语的火焰燃尽尘埃。

心灵，快到此起彼伏的山峦叠嶂里来：
你看神秘的友情正在那里缓缓地盛开
日月交相辉映，幽谷与丛林并肩徘徊
河流与溪水在交汇处携手并展望未来；

上帝吹着号角打着轻巧的节拍，可为何听起来是那么无奈，
看着时光与整个世界一起衰败，奔向未来却永远无法倒带；
可曾想爱情也逐渐黯淡了光彩，暮霭看起来比她更加和蔼，
当希望竟不如朝露看起来可爱，那我又要如何来把爱释怀。

He Tells of the Perfect Beauty

O cloud-pale eyelids, dream-dimmed eyes,

The poets labouring all their days

To build a perfect beauty in rhyme

Are overthrown by a woman's gaze

And by the unlabouring brood of the skies:

And therefore my heart will bow, when dew

Is dropping sleep, until God burn time,

Before the unlabouring stars and you.

他永远的沉鱼落雁

眼睑,白若云烟,双眼,梦落缠绵,

诗人们耗尽最后一滴岁月

想在韵律里留下永远的沉鱼落雁

只不过那夜与佳人相望一眼,从此光阴静止了笔尖

子夜,繁星漫天,心弦,辗转无眠:

我怀抱着全部的心甘情愿

露珠滴落的午夜凋谢了我的梦魇,

我愿沉睡在繁星与你的季节,直到上帝画下了终点。

The Arrow

I thought of your beauty, and this arrow,

Made out of a wild thought, is in my marrow.

There's no man may look upon her, no man,

As when newly grown to be a woman,

Tall and noble but with face and bosom

Delicate in colour as apple blossom.

This beauty's kinder, yet for a reason

I could weep that the old is out of season.

Summer for Thee Grant I May Be

光阴似箭，
莫道从前

我想起你至美的容颜，像一根思念的箭，
满是无法翻篇的怀念，扎进我的骨髓间。
没有一个男人会为她哀怨，无人会留恋，
当年窈窕的你闯入我眼帘，恍若在昨天，
似天仙，流风回雪，慕红颜，风姿绰约
苹果花绽放的娇艳，不如你倾城的侧脸。
如今的你却美得更婉约，虽然我也曾把时光埋怨
你回望从前，我不再挂念，锦瑟何须伤离别，都只如初见。

O Do Not Love Too Long

Sweetheart, do not love too long:

I loved long and long,

And grew to be out of fashion

Like an old song.

All through the years of our youth

Neither could have known

Their own thought from the other's,

We were so much at one.

But O, in a minute she changed—

O do not love too long,

Or you will grow out of fashion

Like an old song.

请别爱得太久

亲爱的,请别爱得太久:
我的爱走过了天长地久,
最后逐渐地淡出了潮流
像无人再听的老歌一首。

在我们青春洋溢的年头
没有谁会想把真相看透
彼此的思想在道尽情柔,
我们曾如此与彼此相守。

然而刹那间便化为乌有——
所以啊,请别爱得太久,
不然你终将被时光赶走
像老歌一首,喋喋不休。

A Song

I thought no more was needed

Youth to prolong

Than dumb-bell and foil

To keep the body young.

O who could have foretold

That the heart grows old?

Though I have many words,

What woman's satisfied,

I am no longer faint

Because at her side?

O who could have foretold

That the heart grows old?

I have not lost desire

But the heart that I had;

I thought 'twould burn my body

Laid on the death-bed,

For who could have foretold

That the heart grows old?

一首心歌

我已不再执着那些幻想
不再渴望能让青春延长
除了哑铃和斑驳的剑芒
还有什么能让身体强壮。
唉，又有谁曾经能想象
我这颗心已经走向荒凉？

纵使我随时能出口成章，
使得女人为我芳心荡漾，
为何我不再迷恋温柔乡
哪怕我仍躺在她的身旁？
唉，又有谁曾经能猜想
我的心早已放下了欲望？

我并未彻底抛弃了渴望
但我的心却遗失在过往；
我曾试想被燃烧的模样
躺在床上等待生命终场，
又有谁能在此刻觉察到我心底的坚强
我这颗逐渐衰老的心依然能为爱吟唱？

但愿我是　你的夏日

A Deep-sworn Vow

Others because you did not keep

That deep-sworn vow have been friends of mine;

Yet always when I look death in the face,

When I clamber to the heights of sleep,

Or when I grow excited with wine,

Suddenly I meet your face.

心的誓言

多情最当年,莫道西风残烟倦薄缘

落花又时节,肠断故情人去心易变;

无常几度人间,料得青衫湿遍,

思梦月如弦,欲踩小楼红阶空凄切,

举杯晓寒天,试把人间风月尽舞遍,

夜末眠,人已远,旧时红颜明月,从此相思绝。

William Wordsworth

威廉·华兹华斯
1770—1850

英国浪漫主义诗人,"湖畔诗人"的代表,被封为桂冠诗人,代表作《咏水仙》。

华兹华斯生于律师之家,父母经常和华兹华斯一起读诗。从小的诗文熏陶,使华兹华斯热爱阅读和诗文创作。不幸的是,母亲在他8岁时过世,父亲在他13岁时过世,但是华兹华斯并未放弃努力,经过自己的刻苦学习,最终在17岁时考入英国剑桥大学。

华兹华斯热爱自然,其所创作的诗文,主题以自然风光为主。在华兹华斯看来,自然是快乐和智慧的源泉,他曾写道:"Let nature be your teacher."(让自然成为你的老师)。他和朋友远离城市,隐居在英格兰湖区,由此得名"湖畔诗人"。他生活朴素,热爱思考,曾写道"plain living and high thinking"(朴素生活,高尚思考)。

William Wordsworth
威廉·华兹华斯

My Heart Leaps Up When I Behold

The Sparrow's Nest

Written in March

To Sleep

To the Cuckoo

Untitled—Scorn Not the Sonnet

Untitled

To—

Untitled

Daffodils

After-Thought

我的心总在荡漾	65
麻雀窝	66
阳春三月，落笔成缘	68
我愿今夜，一念入眠	70
致杜鹃	72
无题——谁敢轻视十四行诗的丰碑	76
无题——英格兰，露西，和我的爱	78
致你的美	80
无题——嫣然一笑，情缘未了	82
咏水仙	84
追思	88

Summer for Thee Grant I May Be

My heart leaps up when I behold

A rainbow in the sky:

So was it when my life began;

So is it now I am a man;

So be it when I shall grow old,

Or let me die!

The child is father of the man:

And I could wish my days to be

Bound each to each by natural piety.

My Heart Leaps Up When I Behold
我的心总在荡漾

我的心总在荡漾

每当欣赏彩虹把天边照亮：

仿佛我小的时候就是这样；

现在长大了也依然一样；

那等我老了也请把同样的剧本奉上，

否则就请让我走向灭亡！

因为孩子其实是成人的榜样：

所以我多么希望我一世苍茫

都紧紧镶嵌着对自然虔诚的神往。

The Sparrow's Nest

Behold, within the leafy shade,

Those bright blue eggs together laid!

On me the chance-discovered sight

Gleamed like a vision of delight.

I started—seeming to espy

The home and sheltered bed,

The Sparrow's dwelling, which, hard by

My Father's house, in wet or dry

My sister Emmeline and I

Together visited.

She looked at it and seemed to fear it;

Dreading, tho' wishing, to be near it:

Such heart was in her, being then

A little Prattler among men.

The Blessing of my later years

Was with me when a boy:

She gave me eyes, she gave me ears;

And humble cares, and delicate fears;

A heart, the fountain of sweet tears;

And love, and thought, and joy.

麻雀窝

快瞧，这绿叶浓密的霓裳，
是谁把这窝青青的鸟蛋悄悄地隐藏！
这偶然遇见的景象
就像是奇妙的幻境在闪闪发光。
于是我开始张望
这个美妙的窝和隐秘的小睡床，
麻雀的小巢就在一旁
紧挨着我父亲的花房，不管潮湿还是干爽
我的妹妹艾米兰都与我经常
一同去把它探望。

她向鸟窝里张望，看起来却有些惊慌；
有些担心却又多想靠近它的身旁：
这是如此的好心肠
专属这位还天真无邪的小姑娘。
从那以后相伴多年的福分的芬芳
原来早已从小与我一同成长：
她打开了我眼眸的轩窗，也把我耳边唱响；
那柔情的关心和纤弱的神伤；
一颗真心，便是甜蜜的泪水在真情流淌；
还有爱，我的思想，和那欢乐的悠扬。

Written in March

The cock is crowing,

The stream is flowing,

The small birds twitter,

The lake doth glitter,

The green field sleeps in the sun;

The oldest and youngest

Are at work with the strongest;

The cattle are grazing,

Their heads never raising;

There are forty feeding like one!

Like an army defeated

The snow hath retreated,

And now doth fare ill

On the top of the bare hill;

The ploughboy is whooping—anon—anon:

There's joy in the mountains;

There's life in the fountains;

Small clouds are sailing,

Blue sky prevailing;

The rain is over and gone!

阳春三月，落笔成缘

你听，雄鸡在那边鸣啼，

你看，溪水也奔流不息，

小鸟吱吱喳喳的背影，

划开了湖面的波光粼粼，

翠绿的原野也在阳光下栖息；

不论是这些年长，还是那些年轻

都在勤劳的汗水里忙得不停；

正在尽情享用美食的牛群，

沉沉地完全不愿把头抬起；

四十头融为一体，像在谦卑地行礼！

这多么像战败的散兵在逃避

是残雪留下的痕迹，

现在被全部困入了绝境

清晰了好久不见的山顶；

耕地里放牛娃们唱起了天籁之音：

山谷便沉醉在这愉悦的欢心；

泉水的源头也翻滚着生机；

被威风打碎的云朵也遨游在天际，

天空用蓝色的画笔素描起天晴；

春雨唤醒了尘世间一切美好的空灵！

A flock of sheep that leisurely pass by,

One after one; the sound of rain, and bees

Murmuring; the fall of rivers, winds and seas,

Smooth fields, white sheets of water, and pure sky;

I have thought of all by turns, and yet do lie

Sleepless! and soon the small birds' melodies

Must hear, first uttered from my orchard trees;

And the first cuckoo's melancholy cry.

Even thus last night, and two nights more, I lay,

And could not win thee, Sleep! by any stealth:

So do not let me wear tonight away:

Without Thee what is all the morning's wealth?

Come, blessed barrier between day and day,

Dear mother of fresh thoughts and joyous health!

To Sleep
我愿今夜，一念入眠

群羊们就这样一个接着一个悠闲地走开，
然后是雨声，接着，是蜜蜂低声的告白
奔腾的河流，微风和浩瀚的大海，
平原，纯白的湖光，和天空纯然的等待；
都在我辗转无眠的脑海里不停地使坏
这彻夜无眠的悲哀！不久那些鸟雀们的欢快
就会从不远的果园树枝头传来；
当然还会有杜鹃鸟哽咽的无奈。
昨夜如此，前夜也一样无法将失眠打败，
睡眠啊，你何时才能潜入进来：
不要让我在今晚依然独自彻夜感慨：
没有你，那清晨的繁荣要如何才能精彩？
来吧，请帮我把今天与明日的界线扒开，
只有你能把清新的思想和健康的身体带来！

但愿我是 你的夏日

O blithe new-comer! I have heard,
I hear thee and rejoice:
O Cuckoo! shall I call thee Bird,
Or but a wandering Voice?

While I am lying on the grass
Thy twofold shout I hear,
From hill to hill it seems to pass,
At once far off and near.

Though babbling only to the vale,
Of sunshine and of flowers,
Thou bringest unto me a tale
Of visionary hours.

Thrice welcome, darling of the Spring!
Even yet thou art to me
No bird, but an invisible thing,
A voice, a mystery;

To the Cuckoo
致杜鹃

新来的朋友！我已经听到，
我听见了你和欢乐的感叹号：
杜鹃啊，我能否亲切地称呼你为希望的飞鸟，
或者是生命和弦里那漫步的小调？

当我静卧在芳草地，亲切的怀抱
仿佛听见两声呼唤划破了云霄，
你看它顺着山脉的背脊随风而飘，
时而离我好近，时而要去哪里来把它寻找。

而你的低吟好像只有山谷才知道，
是赞美阳光的闪耀和花枝的妖娆，
而我也为这动人的声线所倾倒
沉醉在江月年华里这曲动情的离骚。

你是春天里的荣耀，欢迎你的来到！
时至今日，你依然是如此的多娇
你不是一只飞鸟，而是幸福隐形的飘渺，
是音律的灵魂，也是神秘奇幻的瑰宝；

The same in my school days

I listened to; that Cry

Which made me look a thousand ways

In bush, and tree, and sky.

To seek thee did I often rove

Through woods and on the green;

And thou wert still a hope, a love;

Still longed for, never seen.

And I can listen to thee yet;

Can lie upon the plain

And listen, till I do beget

That golden time again.

O blessed Bird! the earth we pace

Again appears to be

An unsubstantial, faery place,

That is fit home for Thee!

仿佛时光回到了从前一切都还未苍老

我心疼地听闻着你们忧伤的祷告

千百次我穷尽全部的目光去寻找

穿梭了草丛，穿透了苍穹，也穿越了每一枝树梢。

世间纷纷扰扰，我依然要在徘徊里把你寻找

不管越过茂密的林海，还是绿野仙踪的舞蹈；

你是播种希望的小鸟，更是爱与幸福的征召；

渴望还在喧嚣，而你仍是岁月里不露痕迹的低调。

我聆听着你的歌声绵延滔滔；

伴奏的是躺卧一旁的原野动情的笙箫

宁静里我听见了时光的心跳

把往昔的流金岁月都回放到与你的今朝。

这天赐的福鸟，大地也跟着奔跑

满世界都点燃起春的热闹

这里不仅是蓬莱仙境里最美的风雨潇潇，

更是人间情柔里，专属于你的美好！

Untitled
—Scorn Not the Sonnet

Scorn not the Sonnet; Critic, you have frowned,

Mindless of its just honours; with this key

Shakespeare unlocked his heart; the melody

Of this small lute gave ease to Petrarch's wound;

A thousand times this pipe did Tasso sound;

With it Camöens soothed an exile's grief;

The Sonnet glittered a gay myrtle leaf

Amid the cypress with which Dante crowned

His visionary brow: a glow-worm lamp,

It cheered mild Spenser, called from Faeryland

To struggle through dark ways; and, when a damp

Fell round the path of Milton, in his hand

The Thing became a trumpet; whence he blew

Soul-animating strains—alas, too few!

无题
——谁敢轻视十四行诗的丰碑

谁敢轻视十四行诗的丰碑；批评家们皱起了双眉，
无须记住它本就有的至美；这把钥匙开启过智慧
莎士比亚用它敞开了心扉；悠扬的旋律让人沉醉
像琵琶带来的柔美把彼特拉克的伤痛轻轻地抚慰；
也像那长笛带来的清脆千百次疗养了塔索的疲惫；
因为它卡蒙斯在流浪的余生里也最终平复了伤悲；
十四行诗闪耀着桃金娘华丽的叶子在摇曳着妩媚
多情的但丁带着柏枝的皇冠尝尽爱情甜蜜的花蕾
在新生里写尽了爱如潮水：它像萤火虫点燃火堆，
温雅的斯宾塞也想入非非，即使仙乡里草长莺飞
他奔赴黑暗的脚步却无悔；当潮湿慢慢地在点缀
把弥尔顿的归途洒满憔悴，他手中的笔不停地挥
涌动的诗篇化作小号劲吹；他高昂地吹奏起光辉
惊心动魄的旋律如影相随——千年成灰的诗情年岁，是否能让我再走一回！

Untitled

I travelled among unknown men,
In lands beyond the sea;
Nor, England! did I know till then
What love I bore to thee.

'Tis past, that melancholy dream!
Nor will I quit thy shore
A second time; for still I seem
To love thee more and more.

Among thy mountains did I feel
The joy of my desire;
And she I cherished turned her wheel
Beside an English fire.

Thy mornings showed, thy nights concealed
The bowers where Lucy played;
And thine too is the last green field
That Lucy's eyes surveyed.

无题
——英格兰，露西，和我的爱

我曾在陌生的人海里行走，
孤独漫步在海那边的尽头；
英格兰那时我才懂了感受
究竟什么才叫作爱得深厚。

时间的背后是梦境在忧愁！
从今以后再不想离你远游
有时候，我会又一次回首
我的爱深刻了每一个春秋。

纯粹的感受在有你的山丘
那宁静的生活在向我挥手；
至爱的她摇着纺车的车轴
依偎在那英式火炉的左右。

朝去暮来光影苒苒在等候
庭院深深有你曾经的嬉游；
漫山遍野的守候是青青芳草爱的温柔
你把永恒藏进露西眼眸里时光的尽头。

但愿我是　你的夏日

To—

Let other bards of angels sing,

Bright suns without a spot;

But thou art no such perfect thing:

Rejoice that thou art not!

Heed not tho'none should call thee fair,

So, Mary, let it be;

If nought in loveliness compare,

With what thou art to me.

True beauty dwells in deep retreats,

Whose veil is unremoved;

Till heart with heart in concord beats,

And the lover is beloved.

致你的美

那就让别的诗人把天使吟唱,
像那完美的太阳一样的晴朗;
然而你怎会是那无瑕的闪光:
我庆幸还好那不是你的模样!

别留意是否无人赞美你漂亮,
亲爱的玛丽,千万别放心上;
人间还有谁能打个美的比方,
你的美已远胜我对美的幻想。

真正的美总会被深深地隐藏,
这幕布要何时才能揭去遮挡;
两颗真心合唱的旋律是爱神的仰望,
我们温暖了时光,然后把彼此爱上。

但愿我是　你的夏日

Untitled 无题
——嫣然一笑,情缘未了

What heavenly smiles! O Lady mine,

Through my very heart they shine;

And, if my brow gives back their light,

Do thou look gladly on the sight;

As the clear Moon with modest pride

Beholds her own bright beams

Reflected from the mountain's side

And from the headlong streams.

红妆嫣然何人笑,

一笑倾城,孤心明月邀;

朝霞如玉映眉梢,

铅华看尽又一宵;

晓月凌空何人照

月华似水,仍似初弦好

群山沉影声渐悄

流水未尽情未老。

Summer for Thee Grant I May Be

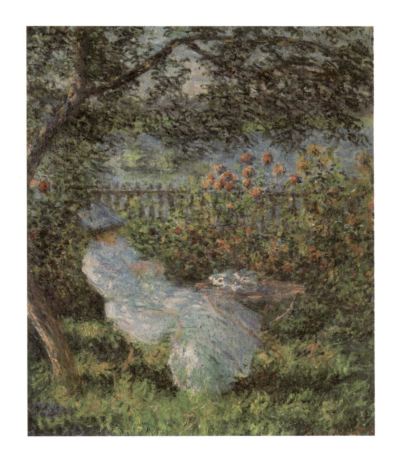

但願我是 你的夏日

I wander'd lonely as a cloud

That floats on high o'er vales and hills,

When all at once I saw a crowd,

A host, of golden daffodils;

Beside the lake, beneath the trees,

Fluttering and dancing in the breeze.

Continuous as the stars that shine

And twinkle on the Milky Way,

They stretch'd in never-ending line

Along the margin of a bay:

Ten thousand saw I at a glance,

Tossing their heads in sprightly dance.

Daffodils
咏水仙

漫步在这无月的孤独，不知归路
多情的云朵也凄美了山谷的云雾，
我蓦然回顾，远处有什么在漂浮，
是金黄的水仙，那样般分外攒簇；
在那湖边，轻轻依偎着绿荫楚楚，
风起云舒，怎能可惜了随风轻舞。

绵延十里仿佛夜空中的星罗棋布
浩瀚的天地挂满了闪亮的夜明珠，
他们并肩排成了延绵不绝的队伍
把湖畔点缀成了彩蝶纷飞的花都：
写意地一瞥便是满目的万朵千株，
随风摇晃的花朵轻踩活力的舞步。

The waves beside them danced, but they

Out-did the sparkling waves in glee:

A poet could not be but gay,

In such a jocund company:

I gazed—and gazed—but little thought

What wealth the show to me had brought:

For oft, when on my couch I lie

In vacant or in pensive mood,

They flash upon that inward eye

Which is the bliss of solitude;

And then my heart with pleasure fills,

And dances with the daffodils.

动情的涟漪也呼应起他们的感触
然而水仙的欢喜却让涟漪更羡慕：
诗人又怎会感应不到欢乐的祝福，
如果他今生某时能有幸身临此处：
我这样凝望着凝望着竟有些恍惚
未曾想美景已赐予了我一生呵护：

那以后每当我躺卧进睡椅的束缚
满心痛苦或是陷入了沉思的虚无，
水仙便会浮现驱散我眼里的迷雾
带我从孤独走向欢声笑语的国度；
摇曳的欢愉掸尽纷扰的悲喜无数，
我与水仙在云间共舞，人间何处。

After-Thought

I thought of Thee, my partner and my guide,

As being past away. —Vain sympathies!

For, backward, Duddon! as I cast my eyes,

I see what was, and is, and will abide;

Still glides the Stream, and shall for ever glide;

The Form remains, the Function never dies;

While we, the brave, the mighty, and the wise,

We Men, who in our morn of youth defied

The elements, must vanish; —be it so!

Enough, if something from our hands have power

To live, and act, and serve the future hour;

And if, as toward the silent tomb we go,

Through love, through hope, and faith's transcendent dower,

We feel that we are greater than we know.

追思

我思念着你,我的伙伴,我的导向,
转身的分别,留下了我无尽的惆怅!
达登河,我聚精会神地在前后瞭望,
看见了过往今日与未来不变的模样;
大江东去的永续是奔流不息的时光;
完全一样的波浪,依然一致的欢畅;
我们的身上,是勇敢、智慧与力量,
年少轻狂是彻夜不眠的心气在逞强
这些终将被时光遗忘,如此又何妨!
我们期望今生我们亲手创造的能量
能留下,滋长,能一样把未来照亮;
当我们某一刻回归寂静的大地土壤,
我们依然守护着那一份爱、希望、坚定而崇高的信仰,
那我们终将变成曾经梦想里更好的模样,对自己仰望。

但愿我是 你的夏日

George Gordon Byron

乔治·戈登·拜伦
1788—1824

英国 19 世纪初期杰出的浪漫主义诗人,与雪莱并称为英国浪漫主义诗歌的"双子星座"。代表作有长篇叙事诗《唐璜》、抒情诗《她走来,洒一路娇美》。

拜伦 10 岁时继承了家族的世袭爵位,成为第六世拜伦勋爵,因此被称为 Lord Byron。拜伦 17 岁时进入剑桥大学学习文学和历史。大学时期的拜伦学习并不刻苦,但是他广泛阅读了欧洲的文学、哲学和历史学著作。

大学毕业后,拜伦离开英国,游历了欧洲和西亚,为以后的诗歌创作打下了基础。拜伦不仅是浪漫主义诗人,也是为理想而战斗一生的勇士,他最终献身于希腊民族解放运动,于 1824 年在希腊病逝。

George Gordon Byron

乔治·戈登·拜伦

To M.S.G

So We'll Go No More A-Roving

She Walks in Beauty

I Saw Thee Weep

When We Two Parted

Stanzas for Music

All Is Vanity, Saith the Preacher

If Sometimes in the Haunts of Men

To a Lady

致 M.S.G	94
我们将不再徘徊	99
她走来，洒一路娇美	100
我见过你潸然泪下	102
当我们天各一方	104
那些音乐的桥段	106
传道者说：往事如烟，万物皆空	108
致倘若人间偶然 误入梦里江南你的美	112
愿你能听见	118

When I dream that you love me, you'll surely forgive;

Extend not your anger to sleep;

For in visions alone your affection can live,—

I rise, and it leaves me to weep.

Then, Morpheus! envelope my faculties fast,

Shed o'er me your languor benign;

Should the dream of tonight but resemble the last,

What rapture celestial is mine!

To 致 M.S.G

如果在梦里你接受了我的爱恋，你千万别埋怨；
千万别把你的满心怒火迁怒于如此无辜的睡眠；
你爱恋的情感只有在我的梦境里才会得以展现，
然而每当我醒来，只有眼泪能陪伴在我的身边。

我想祈愿，睡神赶快封锁我所有的神志与意念，
让你的困倦渗透蔓延，好让我的身体缓缓入眠；
然后再许愿，今夜的梦境接着昨日的剧本重演，
这歌舞升平的天上仙境是我曾朝思暮想的成全！

They tell us that slumber, the sister of death,

Mortality's emblem is given;

To fate how I long to resign my frail breath,

If this be a foretaste of heaven!

Ah! frown not, sweet lady, unbend your soft brow,

Nor deem me to happy in this;

If I sin in my dream, I atone it for now,

Thus doom'd but to gaze upon bliss.

Though in visions, sweet lady, perhaps you may smile,

Oh, think not my penance deficient!

When dreams of your presence my slumbers beguile,

To awake will be torture sufficient.

我曾听说关于睡眠，其实和死亡如同姐妹相连，
那么睡眠是否也可以算作是死亡的另一种表现；
命运之神能否把我的苟延残喘终结得更早一些，
如果天堂里是如此一样的体验，那我真的情愿！

请别皱眉，我亲爱的你，请松弛舒缓你的眉眼，
千万别认为我能从中感受到愉悦或品味到香甜；
梦里我若犯下了罪孽，现在就是我赎罪的时间，
即便我已望穿秋水，幸福也只容许我夜夜思念。

梦里情缘，我知道最亲爱的你一定会笑得很甜，
但愿某天，你不再觉得我的苦行依然缺乏磨炼！
每当入眠，我知道那些与你的美梦只不过是虚假的呈现，
而当梦醒，眼前满是炼狱人间，而我还要再忍受多少年。

但愿我是 你的夏日

Summer for Thee Grant I May Be

So We'll Go No More A-Roving
我们将不再徘徊

So we'll go no more a-roving
So late into the night,
Though the heart be still as loving,
And the moon be still as bright.
For the sword outwears its sheath,
And the soul wears out the breast,
And the heart must pause to breathe,
And Love itself have rest.
Though the night was made for loving,
And the day returns too soon,
Yet we'll go no more a roving
By the light of the moon.

我们将不再徘徊
多情的夜色已晚，
爱神还心潮澎湃，
月光洗尽了无奈。
剑磨去鞘的阻碍，
灵魂把胸膛凿开，
心在沉默中期待，
爱在静谧里留白。
夜原是爱的本来，
白昼转瞬即归还。
我们已不再徘徊
释怀月光的感慨。

She Walks in Beauty

She walks in beauty, like the night

Of cloudless climes and starry skies;

And all that's best of dark and bright

Meet in her aspect and her eyes:

Thus mellowed to that tender light

Which heaven to gaudy day denies.

One shade the more, one ray the less,

Had half impaired the nameless grace

Which waves in every raven tress,

Or softly lightens o'er her face;

Where thoughts serenely sweet express

How pure, how dear their dwelling place.

And on that cheek, and o'er that brow,

So soft, so calm, yet eloquent,

The smiles that win, the tints that glow,

But tell of days in goodness spent,

A mind at peace with all below,

A heart whose love is innocent!

她走来，洒一路娇美

她走来，洒一路娇美
像那无云的夜空零碎，日落星辉；
白与黑，那多情的是非
眼眸里倒映着红颜目翠，柔情似水：
谁在轻柔的光里融进了碾落的青灰
白昼把缘分的思念又留给了谁。

阴影轻声相随，失去了光芒的依偎，
无名的至美也会被写尽枯萎
她那浓密的黑发间满是美的花蕊，
这明眸皓齿的容颜我已写尽千回；
思绪化作宁静里甜蜜的三千弱水
洗礼着她那神圣住所的纯洁高贵。

这瑰丽的脸颊，这迷人的眉，
如此轻柔温婉，是人间至美，
这迷人的笑容是闪耀处色彩的无悔，
久远的过去也解开了我的夜夜除非，
平静的心湖容纳着世间的墨已成碑，
她把心中圣洁的爱写进我诗的结尾！

I Saw Thee Weep

I saw thee weep—the big bright tear

Came o'er that eye of blue;

And then me thought it did appear

A violet dropping dew:

I saw thee smile—the sapphire's blaze

Beside thee ceased to shine;

It could not match the living rays

That filled that glance of thine.

As clouds from yonder sun receive

A deep and mellow dye,

Which scarce the shade of coming eve

Can banish from the sky,

Those smiles unto the moodiest mind

Their own pure joy impart;

Their sunshine leaves a glow behind

That lightens o'er the heart.

我见过你潸然泪下

我见过你潸然泪下，晶莹的泪珠
在湖蓝的眼眸里轻声滑下；
我脑海里的想象满是芳华
冰晶的露水是紫罗兰亲笔的自画：
我见过你笑靥如花，蔚蓝的宝石
被你的柔情黯淡了光泽的典雅；
那灵动的光芒在不远处惊讶
你嫣然的一笑便是人间所有的牵挂。

夕阳披上了云雾走向了远方的天涯
还顺手染上了那最绮丽多姿的晚霞，
即使是微冷的黄昏也只能独自装傻
谁能把它吹向那天际外飘渺的风沙，
你的笑容吻醒了我心底忧伤的枝丫
也轻轻地揭开了那纯真欢乐的面纱；
阳光温柔地把最暖的一束为我留下
心底的爱恋在发芽，与你专属的情话。

When We Two Parted
当我们天各一方

When we two parted
In silence and tears,
Half broken-hearted
To sever for years,
Pale grew thy cheek and cold,
Colder thy kiss;
Truly that hour foretold
Sorrow to this!

The dew of the morning
Sunk chill on my brow;
It felt like the warning
Of what I feel now.
Thy vows are all broken,
And light is thy fame:
I hear thy name spoken
And share in its shame.

昔我过往，子夜离殇
相顾无言，泪已千行，
心灯茫茫，情断肝肠
此去经年，归期何望，
皓颜如雪，却已成霜，
一吻情深，怎奈夜凉；
星河荡漾，道尽天狼
恍若今日，落寞神伤！

朝烟慕光，白露凝霜
润我眉梢，又冷心房；
沉思默想，欲盖弥彰
物是人非，失措仓皇。
地老天荒，湮灭遗忘，
身名此生，沉浮浪荡：
芳名有闻，如音绕梁
我却竟然，羞愧难当。

They name thee before me,
A knell to mine ear;
A shudder comes o'er me—
Why wert thou so dear?
They know not I knew thee
Who knew thee too well:
Long, long shall I rue thee
Too deeply to tell.

In secret we met:
In silence I grieve
That thy heart could forget,
Thy spirit deceive.
If I should meet thee
After long years,
How should I greet thee?—
With silence and tears.

熙熙攘攘，子名远洋，
钟声贯耳，撞我心墙；
战战兢兢，如坐针芒——
我又为何，如此情长？
无人知晓，与你过往
历历在目，素衣红妆：
思念之长，天各一方
情深难辩，无以名状。

幽会一场，月影暗香：
欲言又止，无边惆怅
饮尽斜阳，孤心遗忘，
灵魂黯淡，一夜入荒。
不期而遇，风回流殇
残烟败柳，几度沧桑，
何以开场，我不思量？——
相顾无言，泪已千行。

There be none of Beauty's daughters

With a magic like thee;

And like music on the waters

Is thy sweet voice to me:

When, as if its sound were causing

The charméd ocean's pausing,

The waves lie still and gleaming,

And the lulled winds seem dreaming;

And the midnight moon is weaving

Her bright chain o'er the deep;

Whose breast is gently heaving,

As an infant's asleep:

So the spirit bows before thee,

To listen and adore thee;

With a full but soft emotion,

Like the swell of summer's ocean.

Stanzas for Music

没有任何一个美的女儿可以释然
在你面前有谁敢说自己美丽绚烂；
如同水上飘来的律动在林间婉转
你甜美的声音是我那守望的期盼：
每当这美妙的旋律再次把爱咏叹
沉醉的海洋便把浪花锁进了安然，
涟漪惬意地躺着柔和了波光闪闪，
凛冽的风也渐渐进入了梦的彼岸：

华丽的月光编织起了绵柔的绸缎
用爱在浩瀚的大海深处洒下温暖；
大海的胸膛渐渐地也步入了平缓
像熟睡的婴儿在梦里幸福地期盼：
心灵向你鞠躬致敬那潺潺的浪漫，
静静地在你身旁倾听年华的璀璨；
心底的浓烈与温婉，还在渲染昨夜的情感，
像夏日海上的波澜，美满了我的灯火阑珊。

那些音乐的桥段

All Is Vanity, Saith the Preacher

Fame, wisdom, love, and power were mine,

And health and youth possess'd me;

My goblets blush'd from every vine,

And lovely forms caress'd me;

I sunn'd my heart in beauty's eyes,

And felt my soul grow tender;

All earth can give, or mortal prize,

Was mine of regal splendour.

传道者说：往事如烟，万物皆空

名声智慧爱情和权力我都曾经拥有，
健康与青春也曾经陪伴在我的左右；
我清澈的高脚杯总被葡萄斟满美酒，
风花雪月的情柔点缀了每一次邂逅；
我曾把照亮心房的光融进美的眼眸，
然后感觉灵魂深处涌动着爱的温柔；
所有世间瑰丽的珍宝和极致的享受，
我曾在这帝王般的华贵里无限停留。

I strive to number o'er what days

Remembrance can discover,

Which all that life or earth displays

Would lure me to live over.

There rose no day, there roll'd no hour

Of pleasure unembitter'd;

And not a trapping deck'd my power

That gall'd not while it glitter'd.

The serpent of the field, by art

And spells, is won from harming;

But that which coils around the heart,

Oh! who hath power of charming?

It will not list to wisdom's lore,

Nor music's voice can lure it;

But there it stings for evermore

The soul that must endure it.

我竭尽全力地去回忆那久远的年头
试图一一打开往事尘封已久的卷轴，
此生的点点滴滴里是否藏匿着不朽
能让我愿意倾注一切只为故地重游。
可我竟然发现每天每时都不堪回首
一切欢愉的笑容里都映着茫茫忧愁；
就像世间哪有任何一件华丽的刺绣
闪耀的背后没有残留磨损下的黑手。

田野里的毒蛇总隐蔽在阴暗的泥垢
为防止伤人术士给予了高明的魔咒；
可如果毒蛇盘踞在我们脆弱的心口，
那么又有谁能来帮我们把毒蛇赶走？
它完全无视智慧在它耳边循循善诱，
音乐的美与柔也无法让它浪子回头；
怎知它无情的噬咬终将会无尽无休
灵魂便要忍受永世无法愈合的伤口。

If Sometimes in the Haunts of Men

致倘若人间偶然
误入梦里江南你的美

If sometimes in the haunts of men
Thine image from my breast may fade,
The lonely hour presents again
The semblance of thy gentle shade:
And now that sad and silent hour
Thus much of thee can still restore,
And sorrow unobserved may pour
The plaint she dare not speak before.

倘若偶然在梦里江南的人世间游荡
你的容颜也渐渐地黯淡在我的心上,
每当我即将坠入无尽的落寞与凄凉
你温柔的倩影便会在我脑海里荡漾:
那久远的时光在我的身旁黯然神伤
然后笔尖把与你的过往写满每一行,
无人觉察的忧伤在晚风里低声吟唱
远方飘来的是曾经未敢诉说的情长。

Oh, pardon that in crowds awhile
I waste one thought I owe to thee,
And self-condemnd'd, appear to simle,
Unfaithful to thy memory!
Nor deem that memory less dear,
That then I seem not to repine;
I would not fools should overhear
One sigh that should be wholly thine.

If not the gob'let pass unquaff'd,
It is not drain'd to banish care;
The cup must hold a deadlier draught,
That brings a Lethe for despair.
And could Oblivion set my soul
From all her troubled visions free,
I'd dash to earth the sweetest bowl
That drown'd a single thought of thee.

请原谅我也曾不免迷失在人海茫茫
思念编织的情网本应只有你的模样,
我无比责怪为何有时候还微笑逞强,
怎能淡忘今生与你走过的地老天荒!
我绝没有让回忆被抛弃在岁月沧桑,
也不曾哀怨过今生走过的跌跌撞撞;
我不愿让愚钝的人们听见我的哭腔
我忧伤的微光只愿是你专属的闪亮。

觥筹交错的红光渐渐地模糊了眼眶,
却仍未洗尽我心底冷若冰霜的惆怅;
谁能在我酒杯里加一勺剧毒的糖浆,
让我内心的绝望彻底从心底被消亡。
或许只有遗忘才能打开我灵魂的窗
让它从纷纷扰扰的痛苦镜像中解放,
但我会毫不犹豫砸碎手中这碗甜汤
如果它胆敢弄伤我对你的一念思量。

For wert thou vanish'd from my mind,
Where could my vacant bosom turn?
And who would then remain behind
To honour thine abandon'd Urn?
No, no—it is my sorrow's pride
That last dear duty to fulfill;
Though all the world forget beside,
'Tis meet that I remember still.

For well I know, that such had been
Thy gentle care for him, who now
Unmourn'd shall quit this mortal scene,
Where none regarded him, but thou:
And, oh! I feel in that was given
A blessing never meant for me;
Thou wert too like a dream of Heaven.
For earthly love to merit thee.

如果某天你消失在我心头毫无迹象，
空虚的心灵要如何找回曾经的方向？
那时候还会有谁能停留在这片土壤
用爱和温暖守护在那斑驳的坟墓旁？
我的荣耀在悲怆的伴奏里慷慨激昂
这最后的职责注定是我此生的荣光；
哪怕在多年以后世界早已把你遗忘，
我依然记得有你的每一个春暖夏凉。

因为我比任何人都知道得更为明朗
你对他的心事永远满是温柔与善良
到时候也不会有人去缅怀他的离场，
只有你还会想起他曾经的烟雨微茫：
你点亮我心的烛光散尽我一世彷徨
这些嘉赏是我此生从未期许的奢望；
有你的他乡便是我梦里向往的天堂。
人间至美的向往叫作我爱你的模样。

To a Lady 　愿你能听见

When Man, expell'd from Eden's bowers,

A moment linger'd near the gate,

Each scene recall'd the vanish'd hours,

And bade him curse his future fate.

But, wandering on through distant climes,

He learnt to bear his load of grief;

Just gave a sigh to other times,

And found in busier scenes relief.

Thus, Mary! will it be with me,

And I must view thy charms no more;

For, while I linger near to thee,

I sigh for all I knew before.

In flight I shall be surely wise,

Escaping from temptation's snare;

I cannot view my paradise

Without the wish of dwelling there.

Summer for Thee　Grant I May Be

人类被逐出了无忧无虑的伊甸园，
门外顾盼的眼里满是懊悔在蔓延，
回忆的画面——把时光倒回从前，
未来的香甜也在亏欠里渐行渐远。

而后他流浪在那遥远的天地之间，
感悟了如何忍耐满心的苦不堪言；
一声叹息吹走了绵绵的过往云烟，
漫天的繁星也温暖了心底的深渊。

亲爱的玛丽我多想陪伴在你身边，
昨日的容颜却成了我今日的思念；
如果我还能与你相遇在某个雨天，
我会用诗篇成全曾经所有的抱歉。

转眼间我已抵达了没有你的天边，
试图摆脱被煎熬笼罩的每个午夜；
我放下对天堂的执念，欲写尽人间的一厢情愿
却发现我骄傲的笔尖，迷失在有你的似水流年。

Percy Bysshe Shelley

珀西·比希·雪莱
1792—1822

英国浪漫主义民主诗人、作家和哲学家,被誉为"诗人中的诗人",与拜伦并称为英国浪漫主义诗歌的"双子星座"。

雪莱18岁时入读牛津大学。他喜欢诗歌,也大量阅读自然科学书籍。雪莱24岁离开英国,游历欧洲,先后结识了拜伦和济慈,并与他们成为一生的挚友。

不幸的是,雪莱在一次回家途中遇到海上风暴,不幸遇难,年仅30岁。雪莱生前积极投身革命运动,将内心的情感和自然景物完美结合,写成代表作《西风颂》,其中的"冬天来了,春天还会远吗?"脍炙人口。

Percy Bysshe Shelley
珀西·比希·雪莱

Love's Philosophy

From the Arabic: An Imitation

Time

Time Long Past

A Lament

To—

To—

Remembrance

爱的哲学　　　　　　　　126

爱的模仿　　　　　　　　128

时间　　　　　　　　　　130

那些时光吹远的从前　　　132

一声叹息　　　　　　　　134

致——　　　　　　　　　136

对爱致敬　　　　　　　　138

回忆的模样　　　　　　　140

Percy Bysshe Shelley
珀西·比希·雪莱

Mutability

The Past

Sonnet Untitled

The Indian Serenade

Fragment on Keats

An Exhortation

Sonnet

On a Faded Violet

人生无常	144
那些逝去的	146
真理的寻觅	148
小夜曲	150
有一种诗,名叫济慈	154
告诫	156
十四行诗:如何自处	160
一朵枯萎的紫罗兰	162

The fountains mingle with—the river,

And the rivers with the ocean;

The winds of Heaven mix for ever

With a sweet emotion;

Nothing in the world is single;

All things by a law divine

In one spirit meet and mingle—

Why not I with thine?

See the mountains kiss high Heaven,

And the waves clasp one another;

No sister flower would be forgiven

If it disdained its brother;

And the sunlight clasps the earth,

And the moonbeams kiss the sea:

What is all this sweet work worth,

If thou kiss not me?

Love's Philosophy

泉水与河流的前世与今生，
像江河与大海的一样深沉；
天空刻满了那交织的风痕
我闻到了甜蜜的落叶缤纷；
人间从来不存在孑然一身；
前世便签下了今生的缘分
如果缘分终将在某日重逢——
那么我一人何时变成我们？

我看见山峰在与天空拥吻，
千百叠浪演绎着爱的情深；
没有姐妹花能被宽恕容忍
如果面对手足她面目可憎；
拥抱大地是阳光爱的温存
亲吻大海是月光爱的纯真
如果甜蜜，才是人间的永恒
那么你的吻，可否借我一生？

爱的哲学

From the Arabic: An Imitation

My faint spirit was sitting in the light

Of thy looks, my love;

It panted for thee like the hind at noon

For the brooks, my love.

Thy barb, whose hoofs outspeed the tempest's flight,

Bore thee far from me;

My heart, for my weak feet were weary soon,

Did companion thee.

Ah! fleeter far than fleetest storm or steed

Or the death they bear,

The heart which tender thought clothes like a dove

With the wings of care;

In the battle, in the darkness, in the need,

Shall mine cling to thee,

Nor claim one smile for all the comfort, love,

It may bring to thee.

爱的模仿

我虚弱的灵魂就这样静坐在光里
洒落在光影里的柔情是亲爱的你；
想你的时候像麋鹿沐浴在阳光里
那渴望溪水的焦急一如我在想你。
乘风而去的马蹄转眼已销声匿迹，
而我还在原地被时光埋进尘埃里；
我空虚的脚步疲惫了身后的足迹，
因为我的心早已与你忘记了归期。

呼啸的风或疾驰的马都无法比拟
甚至它们背负的死亡也无法匹及，
满心的瀚海柔情裹着思念的外衣
像舒展的白鸽挥舞着关爱的双翼；
不论陷入战争黑夜还是十万火急，
我的心都将紧贴着给你爱的勇气，
对你我绝对不用真心来换取笑意，
愿我的真心能伴你诗化每个雨季。

Unfathomable Sea! whose waves are years,
Ocean of Time, whose waters of deep woe
Are brackish with the salt of human tears!
Thou shoreless flood, which in thy ebb and flow
Claspest the limits of mortality,
And sick of prey, yet howling on for more,
Vomitest thy wrecks on its inhospitable shore;
Treacherous in calm, and terrible in storm,
Who shall put forth on thee,
Unfathomable Sea?

Time 时间

深不可测的大海！岁月是你波浪的形态，
时间的洪流袭来，悲哀是那浪花在感慨
人类咸咸的泪水在浸染，你也咸涩难耐！
无边无尽的潮水在徘徊，你也心潮澎湃
你紧紧掌控着有限生命里那一切的安排，
虽已厌倦了主宰但仍呼唤着更多的淘汰，
那荒芜的岸边满是被你肆意丢弃的残骸；
平静里暗藏居心叵测风暴时便气急败坏，
有谁该面朝阴霾，奔赴你那残忍的决裁，
一切终将被释怀，在你深不可测的大海？

但愿我是 你的夏日

Time Long Past

Like the ghost of a dear friend dead
Is Time long past.
A tone which is now forever fled,
A hope which is now forever past,
A love so sweet it could not last,
Was Time long past.

There were sweet dreams in the night
Of Time long past:
And, was it sadness or delight,
Each day a shadow onward cast
Which made us wish it yet might last—
That Time long past.

There is regret, almost remorse,
For Time long past.
'Tis like a child's belovèd corse
A father watches, till at last
Beauty is like remembrance, cast
From Time long past.

那些时光吹远的从前

像一缕已故友人的灵魂在云间
是那些时光吹远的从前。
像一抹永远逝去的歌声在哽咽,
像一片后会无期的希望在想念,
像甜蜜的爱情却未能走到终点,
是曾经那些时光吹远的从前。

记得午夜有甜美的梦相伴入眠
在那些时光吹远的从前:
然而不论是伤心还是愉悦,
每天投掷的光影都会向前蔓延
使我们为留住永远许下了心愿——
为了那些时光吹远的从前。

有一种遗憾或者说深深的抱歉,
面对那些时光吹远的从前。
像是孩子美好的身体完好无缺
他的父亲守护在每个日日夜夜
直到美的眷恋被回忆写进永远
来自那些时光吹远的从前,好久之前。

A Lament

O world! O life! O time!

On whose last steps I climb,

Trembling at that where I had stood before;

When will return the glory of your prime?

No more—Oh, never more!

Out of the day and night

A joy has taken flight;

Fresh spring, and summer, and winter hoar

Move my faint heart with grief, but with delight

No more—Oh, never more!

一声叹息

啊!世界百态!一生风采!时光不待!
我正攀爬在最后的台阶奔向人生的舞台,
当我回首往事的痕迹时竟有些难以释怀;
你青春的多姿多彩要何年何月才能归来?
不再——唉,永远不再回来!

远离过白昼也逃避过那黑夜无情的阻碍
满心的愉悦已飞往天边五彩斑斓的云彩;
春夏的百花盛开在伏笔冬天的白雪皑皑
我愿忧伤触动我的心房,但如果是欢快
不再——唉,永远不要再来!

To—

One word is too often profaned
    For me to profane it,
One feeling too falsely disdain'd
    For thee to disdain it;
One hope is too like despair
    For prudence to smother,
And Pity from thee more dear
    Than that from another.

I can give not what men call love;
    But wilt thou accept not
The worship the heart lifts above
    And the Heavens reject not,—
The desire of the moth for the star,
    Of the night for the morrow,
The devotion to something afar
    From the sphere of our sorrow?

致——

有个字眼时常被人们亵渎
那么我又怎能再把它玷污,
有种情感时常被不屑一顾
那你又要如何用爱来呵护;
绝望时常长着希望的面目
谨慎便不得已去抑制约束,
我听见了你那怜悯的倾诉
比别人的听来更发自肺腑。

我说不出人们对爱的解读,
然而你竟会拒绝我的情愫
我奉上的是爱的清风玉露
连上天都不忍置我于不顾,——
你看那飞蛾对星辉的仰慕,
是夜晚对黎明的朝朝暮暮,
人们穷尽一生去寻觅归宿
而你是我今生最痛的领悟?

但愿我是 你的夏日

To—
对爱致敬

When passion's trance is overpast,
If tenderness and truth could last,
Or live, whilst all wild feelings keep
Some mortal slumber, dark and deep,
I should not weep, I should not weep!

It were enough to feel, to see,
Thy soft eyes gazing tenderly,
And dream the rest—and burn and be
The secret food of fires unseen,
Couldst thou but be as thou hast been.

After the slumber of the year
The woodland violets reappear;
All things revive in field or grove,
And sky and sea, but two, which move
And form all others, life and love.

当肆无忌惮的激情已经烟消云散，
如果温柔和真诚依然相约在今晚，
生命的感叹无碍那些狂野的情感
尽管还深深地潜伏着无尽的阴暗，
我便不会让泪水呼唤，不会呼唤！

我看到也感受到了那满满的温婉，
你温柔的眼神里倒映着溪水潺潺，
我梦想用你的花瓣燃尽世间严寒
无形火焰的燃料是梦境里的阑珊，
你能否与昨日一样直到海枯石烂。

四季的轮转给时光送上新的早安
原野上绽放着好久不见的紫罗兰；
林间绿野是万物复苏的生机盎然，
天空与海在期盼，守望曾经山花烂漫的风景依然
生命和爱被点燃，是我今生留给人间最后的温暖。

但愿我是 你的夏日

Remembrance
回忆的模样

Swifter far than summer's flight—

Swifter far than youth's delight—

Swifter far than happy night,

Art thou come and gone—

As the earth when leaves are dead,

As the night when sleep is sped,

As the heart when joy is fled,

I am left lone, alone.

比起夏日的行程更加繁忙——
比起青春的愉悦更加张扬——
比起幸福的夜晚更加匆忙,
就这样来时高昂去时沧桑——
像黄叶飘零在大地的胸膛,
像彻夜无眠在黑夜的漫长,
像欢乐离去时内心的凄凉,
我被岁月遗忘,落寞成霜。

The swallow summer comes again—
The owlet night resumes her reign—
But the wild-swan youth is fain
To fly with thee, false as thou.—
My heart each day desires the morrow;
Sleep itself is turned to sorrow;
Vainly would my winter borrow
Sunny leaves from any bough.

Lilies for a bridal bed—
Roses for a matron's head—
Violets for a maiden dead—
Pansies let my flowers be:
On the living grave I bear
Scatter them without a tear—
Let no friend, however dear,
Waste one hope, one fear for me.

云燕的夏日终将带来时光——
猫头鹰的夜会把骄傲披上——
但野天鹅的青春去了远方
像你一样带走了所有希望。——
我的心每天都把明天盼望;
可梦境转眼便被化作忧伤;
我的冬天又是何等的苍茫
阳光枝叶也只是徒增虚妄。

百合花为新娘奉上了新床——
玫瑰在老妇人的额头绽放——
紫罗兰为少女的逝去悲伤——
那请用这三色花为我写上:
在我永眠的墓旁洒满花香
不要洒下任何动情的泪光——
也别让我的挚友把我念想,
哪怕一丝希望,一抹情殇。

The flower that smiles today
Tomorrow dies.
All that we wish to stay,
Tempts and then flies.
What is this world's delight?
Lightning that mocks the night,
Brief even as bright.

Virtue, how frail it is!
Friendship how rare!
Love, how it sells poor bliss
For proud despair!
But we, though soon they fall,
Survive their joy and all
Which ours we call.

今天花儿的笑容是那样的闪亮
可一切都有可能在明天被埋葬。
那些我们希望永远留下的模样，
都经不住诱惑飞去很远的地方。
什么才算是人世间真正的欢畅
是那划破黑夜苍穹的一道闪光？
虽然很短促但是依然无比明亮。

高尚的美德时常脆弱也不坚强！
真挚的友谊何时才能让我遇上！
爱情把可怜的幸福挂进了橱窗
换回来的又常常是骄傲的绝望！
虽然他们转眼间便会落幕离场，
喧嚣的和声听不出欢乐的哼腔
这就是我们所称的我们的假象。

Mutability
人生无常

Whilst skies are blue and bright,
Whilst flowers are gay,
Whilst eyes that change ere night
Make glad the day,
Whilst yet the calm hours creep,
Dream thou—and from thy sleep
Then wake to weep.

每当蓝天还是如此的晴朗明亮，
每当鲜艳的花朵依然抹着红妆，
每当眼前的一切还未染上夜凉
请尽情享受白日里美好的荡漾，
然而每当宁静的时光缓缓流淌，
某一天晚上，幽梦一场，是谁又敲打我的心房
曾经的忧伤在门外飘荡，我的世界飘满了泪光。

但愿我是　你的夏日

The Past

那些逝去的

Wilt thou forget the happy hours
Which we buried in love's sweet bowers,
Heaping over their corpses cold
Blossoms and leaves, instead of mould?
Blossoms which were the joys that fell,
And leaves, the hopes that yet remain.

Forget the dead, the past? Oh, yet
There are ghosts that may take revenge for it,
Memories that make the heart a tomb,
Regret which glide through the spirit's gloom,
And with ghastly whispers tell
That joy, once lost, is pain.

难道你会把那些幸福的时光统统忘记
在爱的绿荫下我们把它们葬在了这里,
是什么在把它们冰冷的躯体轻轻遮蔽
不是淤泥而是鲜花和绿叶编织的外衣?
鲜花是那些随着时间洗尽铅华的欢喜,
而绿叶是至今犹存的希望坚守的痕迹。

是否能忘记那些早已随风而去的回忆
可它们的灵魂也许会埋怨起你的抛弃,
那时记忆便会在心底荒芜出一片墓地,
悔恨也会潜入你灵魂深处悄悄地隐匿,
时常在无月的夜里,一丝阴森的低语便会在耳边响起
若敢遗弃过往的欢喜,痛苦将洗礼你生命的每个四季。

Sonnet Untitled

Lift not the painted veil which those who live

Call Life: though unreal shapes be pictured there,

And it but mimic all we would believe

With colours idly spread,—behind, lurk Fear

And Hope, twin Destinies; who ever weave

Their shadows, o'er the chasm, sightless and drear.

I knew one who had lifted it—he sought,

For his lost heart was tender, things to love,

But found them not, alas! nor was there aught

The world contains, the which he could approve.

Through the unheeding many he did move,

A splendour among shadows, a bright blot

Upon this gloomy scene, a Spirit that strove

For truth, and like the Preacher found it not.

真理的寻觅

不要去掀开那被人们称为生活的彩画的布帘
所有描绘的那些情节都是完全不真实的画面，
这些看来无比可信的细节是刻意得那么明显
完全是那拙劣的画布在漫不经心地即兴表演
相同的命运却有希望与恐惧两种相反的终点
他们在时光的缝隙里编织着难以分辨的容颜。
我知道有人曾把布帘掀开期待能与真相结缘，
渴望温柔他搁浅的心灵也拥抱爱的蜜语甜言，
怎奈失望再次上演然后岁月也逐渐把他翻篇
他一厢情愿的思念并不是他彼岸的海角天边。
他踏过冷漠的人间也看遍了风华背后的深渊，
好似一个光点降落在幽暗的舞台上若隐若现
我也徘徊在天地之间，只为今生能听见你的真言
传道者说今生人间无缘，那我来世能否与你相见。

150

I arise from dreams of thee

In the first sweet sleep of night,

When the winds are breathing low,

And the stars are shining bright

I arise from dreams of thee,

And a spirit in my feet

Hath led me—who knows how?

To thy chamber window, Sweet!

The Indian Serenade
小夜曲

梦里与你的情缘就这样惊醒了我的指尖
这是入夜以来我第一次闻到夜晚的香甜，
徐徐的晚风此刻也轻轻沉睡在我的屋檐，
天边点点的繁星是否在闪耀着我的思念
梦里与你的情缘就这样惊醒在我的枕边，
恍然间发现有个小精灵在我的脚边出现
他就这样牵着我在午夜里走了好远好远？
转眼间我发现这正是梦里你温柔的窗边！

The wandering airs they faint

On the dark, the silent stream—

The champak odors fall

Like sweet thoughts in a dream;

The nightingale's complaint,

It dies upon her heart;

As I must die on thine,

O, beloved as thou art!

O, lift me from the grass!

I die, I faint, I fail!

Let thy love in kisses rain

On my lips and eyelids pale.

My cheek is cold and white, alas!

My Heart beats loud and fast;—

Oh! press it close to thine own again,

Where it will break at last.

风中四处摇曳的歌声听起来已有些疲倦
在想你的午夜也终于同幽静的溪水共眠——
那金香木的香味渐渐地迷失在夜的梦魇
如同梦里与你的蜜语甜言也会消失不见；
夜莺多情的哀怨在夜里是那么揪人心弦，
然后与她心中所有的爱恋一起冷冷湮灭；
既然我也终将告别人间在某个角落长眠，
那我多么希望这个地点就叫作你的思念！

扶我在落寞的草地上站起来再看看人间！
我终将在无尽的眷恋里昏迷在某个阴天！
祈愿上天能把你的爱化作吻的细雨绵绵
落在我苍白的嘴唇和眼眸上模糊了视线。
我的脸颊逐渐冰冷苍白恍惚看见了从前！
我听见心跳声在讲述着那天的惊鸿一瞥；——
如果时光可以倒回到故事的起点，与你遇见的那天，
那我依然只想凋零在想你的午夜，如此悦耳的失眠。

Fragment on Keats

有一种诗，名叫济慈

'Here lieth One whose name was writ on water.'
But, ere the breath that could erase it blew,
Death, in remorse for that fell slaughter,
Death, the immortalizing winter, flew
Athwart the stream, —and time's printless torrent frew
A scroll of cystal, blazoning the name
Of adonais!

"在这里长眠着一个姓名被刻写在水上的人。"
可还没等到远方吹来那试图抹尽它的清风，
死神便已经开始对他的残忍感到懊悔万分，
于是他披上了在那永生冬夜里散发的寒冷
以翱翔的姿态横穿江河在空中吻下了永恒
时光的洪流像那水晶的卷轴在闪耀里奔腾
原来诗神阿多尼便是今生叫作济慈的诗人！

An Exhortation

告诫

Chameleons feed on light and air:

Poets' food is love and fame:

If in this wide world of care

Poets could but find the same

With as little toil as they,

Would they ever change their hue

As the light chameleons do,

Suiting it to every ray

Twenty times a day?

阳光和微风的金枝玉露专属于那珍贵的变色龙：
就像诗人们的粮食是美满的爱情和至高的光荣：
假如这个广阔无边的世界能有同样伟大的宽容
让诗人们也能像珍贵的变色龙一样享受到专宠
诗咏里一切要素的供给都可以变得那样的轻松，
那么他们是否也会去经常适应不同颜色的妆容
就像变色龙在不同的光线下模样也会迥然不同，
为了适应每束光线他们将不得不遭遇困难重重
一日内也许就要变换二十次面孔丝毫不敢放松？

但愿我是 你的夏日

Poets are on this cold earth,

As chameleons might be,

Hidden from their early birth

In a cave beneath the sea;

Where light is, chameleons change:

Where love is not, poets do:

Fame is love disguised: if few

Find either, never think it strange

That poets range.

Yet dare not stain with wealth or power

A poet's free and heavenly mind:

If bright chameleons should devour

Any food but beams and wind,

They would grow as earthly soon

As their brother lizards are.

Children of a sunnier star,

Spirits from beyond the moon,

O, refuse the boon!

诗人们在世间的停留会经历无数个冷漠的寒冬，
即使是变色龙也一样无法绝对避免环境的捉弄，
如果那一刻敲响了世间每一个生命诞辰的时钟
便会发现它们就栖息在那个海底最深处的穴洞；
可每当有光线的时候变色龙就立即披上了彩虹：
倘若没有了爱的呵护诗人便将奔赴他乡的天空：
那些所谓的光荣也不过是爱佩戴的另一副面孔
若两者都消逝在茫茫的虚空那也不必忧心忡忡
诗人们依然会在某个江畔看见他们的万紫千红。

切记千万不能让财富或权力的欲望扎根在心中
诗人们那自由和神圣的心灵便将永远无法歌颂：
倘若某天变色龙被其他看似美味的食物给怂恿
放弃了那些所有曾给予他的阳光和微风的专供，
他们便将坠入尘世间用最迅速的成长奔向平庸
直到最后变得与他们的兄弟蜥蜴一样完全相同。
行走在明媚的天地间是诗人们今生天赐的恩宠，
时光匆匆，夜色正浓，曾经的懵懂已然在灿烂的星空，消失得无影无踪，
风情万种，有恃无恐，怎奈无动于衷方得世间所有的感动，又有谁能懂！

Ye hasten to the grave! What seek ye there,

Ye restless thoughts and busy purposes

Of the idle brain, which the world's livery wear?

Oh thou quick Heart which pantest to possess

All that pale Expectation feigneth fair!

Thou vainly curious mind which wouldest guess

Whence thou didst come, and whither thou must go,

And all, that never yet was known, wouldst know;

O whither hasten ye, that thus ye press

With such swift feet life's green and pleasant path

Seeking alike from happiness and woe

A refuge in the cavern of gray death?

O Heart, and Mind and Thoughts, what thing do you

Hope to inherit in the grave below?

Sonnet
十四行诗：
如何自处

你们急速奔向坟墓是为寻找什么宝物，
我看见了那躁动的思想和忙碌的意图
你们空虚的大脑难道是尘世间的奴仆？
你迫切的心里是对拥有的欲望在追逐
一切的美好都只是苍白的期望在嫉妒！
你充满好奇的心智总想猜出一切事物
包括你从哪里走来最终又要前往何处，
一切无从知晓的秘密你都想要去揭露；
我惊叹你们就这样疾步向着远方奔赴
人间愉快的绿荫大道你们也不睬不顾
不清楚你们是渴望快乐还是寻求痛苦
灰色死亡的洞穴能帮你解脱还是庇护？
人们的内心、头脑和思想为何执着于飘渺虚无，我竟有些迷糊
地下坟墓里你们又将会获得什么宝物？恍惚，我又该如何自处？

On a Faded Violet

The odour from the flower is gone
Which like thy kisses breathed on me;
The colour from the flower is flown
Which glowed of thee and only thee!

A shrivelled, lifeless, vacant form,
It lies on my abandoned breast,
And mocks the heart which yet is warm,
With cold and silent rest.

I weep, —my tears revive it not!
I sigh, —it breathes no more on me;
Its mute and uncomplaining lot
Is such as mine should be.

一朵枯萎的紫罗兰

这朵鲜花的芬芳早已在岁月里消失散尽
如同你的吻倾吐的甜蜜温馨过我的曾经；
这朵鲜花的色泽也在时光里缓缓地凋零
曾经的光影里只有你的身影和你的柔情！

这个早已枯萎、毫无生气的空虚的外形，
就这样倚靠在我被人冷落的胸口间寂静，
嘲弄着我那颗依旧火热的心，满是多情，
是它用冷漠和幽静在我心里勾勒着不幸。

我已然哭尽，然而泪水却无法将它唤醒！
我叹息难平，它将无法再向我吐露真情；
它依然静默无音，往事泪零，可却无意去埋怨那命运的无情
人间芳菲何处寻，总负多情，孤心终将梦醒，早已命中注定。

William Shakespeare

威廉·莎士比亚

1564—1616

英国剧作家、诗人,文艺复兴时期最有代表性的作家之一。莎士比亚著作等身,留存至今的共有 37 部剧本、2 首长诗和 154 首十四行诗(其中最著名的是第 18 首十四行诗)。

莎士比亚第一个打破了悲剧和喜剧的界限,他的戏剧创作来源于民间故事;他的戏剧语言融合了文学语言和民间语言,生动又贴近生活。代表作有《哈姆雷特》《罗密欧与朱丽叶》《麦克白》《李尔王》等。

在西方文学史上,有两个人并列为双峰——但丁和莎士比亚。

William Shakespeare
威廉·莎士比亚

Sonnet 5

Sonnet 8

Sonnet 18

Sonnet 21

Sonnet 29

Sonnet 32

Sonnet 54

Sonnet 60

Sonnet 63

Sonnet 64

Sonnet 65

第 5 首　十四行诗　　　　　　　170

第 8 首　十四行诗　　　　　　　172

第 18 首　十四行诗　　　　　　174

第 21 首　十四行诗　　　　　　176

第 29 首　十四行诗　　　　　　178

第 32 首　十四行诗　　　　　　180

第 54 首　十四行诗　　　　　　182

第 60 首　十四行诗　　　　　　184

第 63 首　十四行诗　　　　　　186

第 64 首　十四行诗　　　　　　188

第 65 首　十四行诗　　　　　　190

William Shakespeare
威廉·莎士比亚

Sonnet 73

Sonnet 74

Sonnet 76

Sonnet 83

Sonnet 94

Sonnet 103

Sonnet 105

Sonnet 116

Sonnet 122

Sonnet 129

Sonnet 150

第 73 首	十四行诗	192
第 74 首	十四行诗	194
第 76 首	十四行诗	196
第 83 首	十四行诗	198
第 94 首	十四行诗	202
第 103 首	十四行诗	204
第 105 首	十四行诗	206
第 116 首	十四行诗	208
第 122 首	十四行诗	210
第 129 首	十四行诗	212
第 150 首	十四行诗	214

Those Hours that with gentle work did frame

The lovely gaze where every eye doth dwell

Will play the tyrants to the very same,

And that unfair which fairly doth excel.

For never-resting time leads summer on

To hideous Winter and confounds him there;

Sap check'd with frost and lusty leaves quite gone,

Beauty o'ersnowed and bareness everywhere;

Then were not summer's distillation left,

A liquid prisoner pent in walls of glass,

Beauty's effect with beauty were bereft,

Nor it, nor no remembrance what it was.

But flowers distilled, though they with winter meet,

Leese but their show; their substance still lives sweet.

Sonnet 5

第 5 首 十四行诗

往事云烟把最柔美的裁剪留给了今天
明眸笑颜是每一行针眼里编织的思念
刹那间全被无情岁月撕成了满地碎片,
昙花一现的背后是沉淀的至美被翻篇。
不舍昼夜的时光拉着夏日奔向了天边
万籁俱寂的寒冬在悄悄地回望着从前;
我看着青青绿叶被千年冰霜封进山岩,
美也被白雪埋进荒芜的原野再也不见;
倘若没有在盛夏的屋檐把那精华提炼,
没有把美的芳醇锁进晶莹剔透的心间,
一切美的似岁流年也会被冷酷地拦截,
那时还能去哪里荡起回忆里美的秋千。
花儿萃取了春天,那又何怕漫漫冬夜里辗转无眠,
冰雪凋谢了人间,但是花香依然在温暖我的诗篇。

但愿我是 你的夏日

Music to hear, why hear'st thou music sadly?

Sweets with sweets war not, joy delights in joy;

Why lov'st thou that which thou receiv'st not gladly,

Or else receiv'st with pleasure thine annoy?

If the true concord of well-tuned sounds

By unions married, do offend thine ear,

They do but sweetly chide thee, who confounds

In singleness the parts that thou shouldst bear:

Mark how one string, sweet husband to another,

Strikes each in each by mutual ordering,

Resembling sire, and child, and happy mother,

Who all in one, one pleasing note do sing:

Whose speechless song being many, seeming one,

Sings this to thee: 'Thou single wilt prove none.'

Sonnet 8

第 8 首　十四行诗

耳边音律的纷争，听起来为何有些微冷？
甜蜜把甜蜜封存，欢笑的背面满是伤痕；
是什么让你心疼，不能让喜悦散尽黄昏，
是什么让你转身，在苦闷的旋律里静等？
如果越听越伤人，哪怕如此和谐的剧本
每当旋律在低声，能否听见这爱的诚恳，
悠扬诉说的稚嫩，何尝不是呵护你自尊
它多想让你承认，独身终将是有缘无份：
这琴弦上的指纹，在另一端抚琴的良人，
乐谱上满是认真，因为灵魂把生命共振，
幸福背后的年轮，是一家三口爱的永恒，
希望你终将听闻，爱与岁月风痕的和声：
悠扬的音准，一曲缘分已道尽人间所有的爱恨，
耳边的回声，"一往情深终究只是我一人的天真"。

Shall I compare thee to a Summer's day?
Thou art more lovely and more temperate:
Rough winds do shake the darling buds of May,
And Summer's lease hath all too short a date:
Sometime too hot the eye of heaven shines,
And often is his gold complexion dimm'd;
And every fair from fair sometime declines,
By chance, or nature's changing course, untrimm'd;
But thy eternal Summer shall not fade,
Nor lose possession of that fair thou ow'st;
Nor shall Death brag thou wander'st in his shade,
When in eternal lines to time thou grow'st:
So long as men can breathe, or eyes can see,
So long lives this, and this gives life to thee.

Sonnet 18

第 18 首　十四行诗

要用多美的文笔才能把你写进夏日里？
你早已突破了我对可爱和柔情的定义：
漫天飞舞的花蕾沉睡在五月的晚风里，
微凉的秋紧盯着夏日的沙漏所剩无几：
要怎样热情的光才能从天边照到这里，
再美的容颜也会时常经历黯淡的洗礼；
一切的美好都存在梦境与现实的距离，
生命无常的漫不经心也怎奈情非得已；
但你那永恒夏日的点滴终将不被忘记，
就像你的美永远刻进了爱神的时光机；
生命的休止符也无法将你画入阴影里，
因为你早已是那岁月如歌的诗情画意：
只要遥远的天际还能听见心动的呼吸，
一定是我在永恒岁月里与此诗在等你。

但愿我是　你的夏日

So is it not with me as with that Muse,

Stirr'd by a painted beauty to his verse,

Who heaven itself for ornament doth use,

And every fair with his fair doth rehearse,

Making a couplement of proud compare

With sun and moon, with earth and sea's rich gems,

With April's first-born flowers and all things rare

That heaven's air in this huge rondure hems;

O let me true in love but truly write,

And then believe me, my love is as fair

As any mother's child, though not so bright

As those gold candles fixed in heaven's air:

Let them say more than like of hearsay well,

I will not praise, that purpose not to sell.

Sonnet 21

第 21 首　十四行诗

我与那位诗人有截然不同的观点，
他一见到浓妆美人就要歌颂美艳，
把她的饰品称为上天恩赐的香甜，
道尽所有的美只为描绘她的容颜，
用各种夸张的对比来渲染着爱恋
比如日月辉映与海陆精华的情缘，
抑或是四月的鲜花那娇嫩的新鲜
与星球大气层范围里一切的罕见；
让我忠于爱但依然去真心地展现，
请相信我描写的一切对你的感言
与任何母亲的孩子一样美若天仙
却比不上天边金烛台的那般光艳：
那就让他们尽情地去卖弄拙劣浮夸的字眼，
我最纯净的笔尖只会速写与你邂逅的从前。

但愿我是　你的夏日

Sonnet 29

第 29 首　十四行诗

When in disgrace with Fortune and men's eyes

I all alone beweep my outcast state,

And trouble deaf heav'n with my bootless cries,

And look upon myself, and curse my fate,

Wishing me like to one more rich in hope,

Featured like him, like him with friends possessed,

Desiring this man's art and that man's scope,

With what I most enjoy contented least;

Yet in these thoughts myself almost despising,

Haply I think on thee, and then my state,

Like to the lark at break of day arising,

From sullen earth sings hymns at heaven's gate;

For thy sweet love remembered such wealth brings

That then I scorn to change my state with kings.

当我失去了幸福,也惨遭旁人白眼的羞辱
我只能走入孤独,哭诉我再次被他人驱逐,
我曾试图借无用的哭泣向耳聋的苍天求助,
顾影自怜只能埋怨命运为何对我如此残酷,
我多希望我也能如他人一样前途风雨无阻,
或者像其他才俊总是高朋满座谈笑尽鸿儒,
我渴望他的气质与艺术和他的眼界与深度,
平时的引以为傲我却给了最不满意的评估;
但是就在我即将于绝望自负的深渊里迷路,
我的脑海里浮现出你的面目,似人间朝暮,
好像那破晓时分的云燕冲向天空云卷云舒,
天边传来那悠扬的歌声唤醒了我心底深处;
你的爱甜蜜了我回忆的幽谷,幽谷里满是与你的专属情愫
人间风雨无数,不知归路,试问皇都应何处,却道有情无。

但愿我是 你的夏日

If thou survive my well-contented day,

When that churl death my bones with dust shall cover,

And shalt by fortune once more re-survey

These poor rude lines of thy deceased lover:

Compare them with the bett'ring of the time,

And though they be outstripped by every pen,

Reserve them for my love, not for their rhyme,

Exceeded by the height of happier men.

O then vouchsafe me but this loving thought,

'Had my friend's Muse grown with this growing age,

A dearer birth than this his love had brought,

To march in ranks of better equipage:

But since he died and poets better prove,

Theirs for their style I'll read, his for his love.'

Sonnet 32

第 32 首 十四行诗

如果我的生命之泉即将缓缓地被流尽，
世间的尘土还在为我摇晃思念的风铃，
哪天你偶然拾起了翻阅我诗歌的心情
我潦草的字迹里你会发现我们的感应：
那时候请你轻轻翻开其他跳动的笔名，
炫丽的文笔是诗人们高声炫耀的作品，
可我只愿你拥抱我诗里的每一分真心，
我知道论技巧我远没有那时候的高明。
我猜亲爱的你也许会听见爱神的声音，
"若我的诗咏也能有幸与时代并肩同行，
那我会让新时代的赞美不再空有其名，
在时光的迷宫里我的柔情会历久弥新：
当生命走向了寂静，诗人们张扬起文笔的天性，
他们还在渲染空灵，而我的诗里只有你的天晴"。

Sonnet 54

第54首　十四行诗

O how much more doth beauty beauteous seem,

By that sweet ornament which truth doth give!

The rose looks fair, but fairer we it deem

For that sweet odour which doth in it live.

The canker-blooms have full as deep a dye

As the perfumed tincture of the roses,

Hang on such thorns and play as wantonly

When summer's breath their masked buds discloses:

But, for their virtue only is their show,

They live unwoo'd and unrespected fade,

Die to themselves. Sweet roses do not so;

Of their sweet deaths are sweetest odours made:

And so of you, beauteous and lovely youth,

When that shall fade, my verse distils your truth.

Summer for Thee Grant I May Be

哦，原来美可以被放大到如此的细致入微，
这多少倍至美的背后原来是真添加的光辉！
你看这玫瑰的美是多么迷人多么爱彻心扉
可无知的我们不知原来更美的是她的香味。
我们看着远处那绮丽的深红渲染的野蔷薇
还错误地把野蔷薇和玫瑰深情地混为一类，
骄傲的我们还在红叶四飞的山水画里沉醉
尤其当夏日炽热的呼吸吹开了每一颗蓓蕾：
但没有人觉察到外表的相似无法看清真伪，
盛开时无人去疼爱凋谢也无人记住她的美，
而玫瑰却给无法阻止的流逝之悲抹去眼泪；
那芬芳隽永的香水味就是生命最好的安慰：
怎奈岁月的轻灰缓缓地下坠遮掩了你的美，
这墨笔尘缘便是你在我诗咏里最美的纯粹。

但愿我是 你的夏日

Like as the waves make towards the pebbled shore,

So do our minutes hasten to their end,

Each changing place with that which goes before,

In sequent toil all forwards do contend.

Nativity, once in the main of light,

Crawls to maturity, wherewith being crowned

Crooked eclipses' gainst his glory fight,

And Time, that gave, doth now his gift confound.

Time doth transfix the flourish set on youth,

And delves the parallels in beauty's brow;

Feeds on the rarities of nature's truth,

And nothing stands but for his scythe to mow.

And yet to times in hope my verse shall stand,

Praising thy worth, despite his cruel hand.

Sonnet 60

第 60 首　十四行诗

如同那奔向沙滩滚滚执着的海浪，
我们的时光也在静默里走向灭亡，
后浪踩着前人的脚印转身即离场，
我在竞相追逐里静听时光的匆忙。
生命的诞辰轻轻地洒下一束微光，
在爱与恨的终场必将把皇冠戴上
要怎样才能摆脱日蚀无情的逞强，
把岁月的赠礼归还然后随意埋葬。
时光的泉水终将卸下青春的彩妆，
然后在眉宇间留下那深情的过往；
在过往的吞噬里自然也仍在彷徨，
一切的美好都将被时光发配流浪。
我的诗章将与你一同把未来的美酒满上，
用温润的美撕开岁月魔掌下冷酷的伪装。

但愿我是　你的夏日

Against my love shall be as I am now,

With time's injurious hand crushed and o'erworn;

When hours have drained his blood, and fill'd his brow

With lines and wrinkles; when his youthful morn

Hath travailed on to age's steepy night,

And all those beauties whereof now he's king

Are vanishing or vanished out of sight,

Stealing away the treasure of his spring;

For such a time do I now fortify

Against confounding age's cruel knife,

That he shall never cut from memory

My sweet love's beauty, though my lover's life.

His beauty shall in these black lines be seen,

And they shall live, and he in them still green.

Sonnet 63
第 63 首　十四行诗

我爱的人将来也会步入我现在的境地，
也会惨遭时光毒手被揉碎与磨损相逼；
当时光慢慢地饮尽她血液的一点一滴
并在他的额头上刻满条条皱纹的痕迹
他青春的黎明也走向岁月沧桑的夜里，
如今他是一国之君坐拥全部这些美丽
但美丽也将褪色最终被淘汰进虚空里，
并且偷尽他春天里全部那些钻石玉器；
为了那个时期我即刻为堡垒打起地基
来抵御岁月那残忍的刀斧突然间来袭，
那么他将永远无法触及最甜蜜的回忆
满是你的柔美，即便生命终将被遗弃。
灵动的墨笔在淘气，与你在我的诗歌里嬉戏，
时光永远无法抛弃，每一个有你盛开的夏季。

但愿我是　你的夏日

When I have seen by time's fell hand defac'd

The rich proud cost of outworn buried age;

When sometime lofty towers I see down rased

And brass eternal slave to mortal rage;

When I have seen the hungry ocean gain

Advantage on the kingdom of the shore,

And the firm soil win of the wat'ry main,

Increasing store with loss, and loss with store;

When I have seen such interchange of state,

Or state itself confounded, to decay,

Ruin hath taught me thus to ruminate:

That time will come and take my love away.

This thought is as a death, which cannot choose

But weep to have that which it fears to lose.

Sonnet 64

第 64 首 十四行诗

我曾经见过时间那丑陋残酷的手掌
摧毁了无数岁月里奇珍异宝的脸庞；
那高耸的塔楼也被夷成了一片苍茫
连不朽的铜像也逃不过被世界遗忘；
我也曾见过那沟壑难填的无尽海洋
全副武装地把陆地王国的地盘争抢，
可陆地也在大海的侵蚀下奋力抵抗，
盈亏与得失还原了每一次你来我往；
我看到了自然的大屏幕在循环播放，
也看到了庄严的景象被慢慢地埋葬，
这断壁残垣让我如何不用心去思量：
我的爱终将抵不过似水流年的勉强。
可时光用世事无常侵蚀了我的思想
泪光里依然只想把你的手紧紧牵上。

但愿我是　你的夏日

Since brass, nor stone, nor earth, nor boundless sea,

But sad mortality o'er-sways their power,

How with this rage shall beauty hold a plea,

Whose action is no stronger than a flower?

O, how shall summer's honey breath hold out

Against the wrackful siege of batt'ring days

When rocks impregnable are not so stout,

Nor gates of steel so strong, but time decays?

O fearful meditation! Where, alack,

Shall time's best jewel from time's chest lie hid?

Or what strong hand can hold his swift foot back,

Or who his spoil o'er beauty can forbid?

O none, unless this miracle have might:

That in black ink my love may still shine bright.

Sonnet 65
第 65 首 十四行诗

谁曾想铜器磐石大地和一望无际的大海，
都不得不在无常面前把高傲的头低下来，
美又如何才能抵挡住这气势汹汹的主宰，
她的活力看起来还没有一朵鲜花有气概？
夏日里甜蜜的芳香要怎样才能面对天灾
多少日夜猛烈的围攻是命运无情的安排
不论是顽强的磐石一块还是大门的钢材，
都抵不过时间的巨力把一切都碾为尘埃？
要多么可怕的领悟才能发现时光在使坏，
岁月的珍宝终将被隐藏进宝箱不受青睐？
要怎样的巨手才能跟得上他奔跑的节拍，
或者又有谁能允许他挟持美的双手松开？
如果还有谁能带来大洋彼岸希望的等待；
只有你爱的妙手才能让翰墨的黑夜释怀。

但愿我是　你的夏日

That time of year thou mayst in me behold,

When yellow leaves, or none, or few, do hang

Upon those boughs which shake against the cold,

Bare ruined choirs, where late the sweet birds sang;

In me thou seest the twilight of such day

As after sunset fadeth in the west,

Which by and by black night doth take away,

Death's second self that seals up all in rest;

In me thou seest the glowing of such fire

That on the ashes of his youth doth lie,

As the deathbed whereon it must expire,

Consumed with that which it was nourished by;

This thou perceiv'st, which makes thy love more strong,

To love that well, which thou must leave ere long.

Sonnet 73

第 73 首 　十四行诗

或许你已从我眼里觉察到了这个秋季，
如今零碎的黄叶道尽了我的惨惨戚戚
仅有的几片把慌乱无助也抖进寒风里，
这荒凉的歌坛也不再有唱诗鸟来栖息；
或许我眼里的倒影只剩下夕阳残照里
最后的微光也被缓缓埋进了西边天际，
接着夜神便悄悄拾尽大地所有的秘密，
用冷酷无情把一切封存进无声的哭泣；
或许我的眼里仍留有余烬残存的踪迹
无奈青春在烛火摇曳里怎与时光为敌，
像躺在倒计时的病床上写下曲终别离，
过往滋养它的一切也逃不过奄奄一息；
当你看到了这里，我不知你的心里是否下起了雨滴，
我知道后会无期，却不知你心底是否还有我的足迹。

But be contented when that fell arrest

Without all bail shall carry me away;

My life hath in this line some interest,

Which for memorial still with thee shall stay.

When thou reviewest this, thou dost review

The very part was consecrate to thee;

The earth can have but earth, which is his due,

My spirit is thine, the better part of me;

So then thou hast but lost the dregs of life,

The prey of worms, my body being dead,

The coward conquest of a wretch's knife,

Too base of thee to be remembered:

The worth of that, is that which it contains,

And that is this, and this with thee remains.

Sonnet 74

第74首 十四行诗

千万不要担心那岁月无情的捕快
无法抗拒的抓捕总有一天会到来；
我把生命的一半藏进我诗的节拍，
回忆的徘徊终将会在你心底澎湃。
当你抖去墨迹上尘封多年的暮霭
潦草运笔间是我全部生命的精彩；
这人间的微粒终究是大地的尘埃，
灵魂的豪迈在你彼岸的烟雨楼台；
千万不要在意我空空如也的残骸，
终究会被自然埋进那厚厚的青苔，
冥冥中的时光之刃亲手把我淘汰，
把躯体嵌进你记忆里消逝的雾霾：
请不要害怕，灵魂不会让躯体承载悲哀，
那就这样吧，诗的结尾我永远与你同在。

Why is my verse so barren of new pride,

So far from variation or quick change?

Why with the time do I not glance aside

To new-found methods, and to compounds strange?

Why write I still all one, ever the same,

And keep invention in a noted weed,

That every word doth almost tell my name,

Showing their birth, and where they did proceed?

O know, sweet love, I always write of you,

And you and love are still my argument:

So all my best is dressing old words new,

Spending again what is already spent:

For as the sun is daily new and old,

So is my love still telling what is told.

Sonnet 76

第 76 首 十四行诗

为什么我的诗没有染上浓艳的红妆，
在峰回路转的潮流里仍然逆流而上？
为什么我不将他人华丽的诗歌模仿
从不追求惊艳的夸张和技巧的新腔？
为什么我还在把同样的主题给吟唱，
把爱的遐想全写进亘古不变的诗章，
字里行间都能清晰地看到我的模样，
还能遥望那来时的方向和爱的故乡？
亲爱的你知道我的诗从来不会撒谎，
你和爱的主题就是我永恒诗的远方：
所以我要施展全部推陈出新的能量，
把兀自成霜的旧词都洒满鸟语花香：
　既然日月苍茫是新与旧的幽梦一场，
　我的爱与昨日的情长依然如诗一样。

I never saw that you did painting need,

And therefore to your fair no painting set,

I found, or thought I found, you did exceed

The barren tender of a poet's debt;

And therefore have I slept in your report,

That you yourself being extant, well might show

How far a modern quill doth come too short,

Speaking of worth, what worth in you doth grow.

This silence for my sin you did impute,

Which shall be most my glory, being dumb;

For I impair not beauty, being mute,

When others would give life, and bring a tomb.

There lives more life in one of your fair eyes

Than both your poets can in praise devise.

Sonnet 83
第 83 首　十四行诗

我从不承认你的美貌需要添脂抹粉，
所以我放弃了修饰只保留你的纯真，
我发现或者说我自以为发现的口吻
远胜那诗人笔下枯燥无味的抒情文；
于是我选择长眠在你的时间里静等，
好让你自己来讲述最美的日月星辰
再好的羽毛也无法书写下你的情深，
更无法描绘出美德在你心中的芳醇。
你误解了我的沉默不是爱的不诚恳，
我的无声反倒成就了我的荣耀一生；
因为美在默不作声里才能完好无损，
别人写尽一生却把你的美推入黄昏。
你明眸闪烁的岁月之吻惊醒了我的清梦
无数赞美的吻痕都揉进了你的梦醒时分。

They that have power to hurt and will do none,

That do not do the thing they most do show,

Who, moving others, are themselves as stone,

Unmoved, cold, and to temptation slow;

They rightly do inherit heaven's graces

And husband nature's riches from expense;

They are the lords and owners of their faces,

Others but stewards of their excellence.

The summer's flower is to the summer sweet,

Though to itself it only live and die,

But if that flower with base infection meet,

The basest weed out-braves his dignity;

For sweetest things turn sourest by their deeds;

Lilies that fester smell far worse than weeds.

Sonnet 94
第94首 十四行诗

有种人，只手翻天却没想过去加害，
人们的胡猜也不是他们行善的阻碍，
给周遭带来温暖自己确是冰石一块，
冷若冰霜地把无尽的诱惑熬成无奈；
他们才配得上天生丽质天赐的等待
把自然的宝贵财富点点滴滴地安排；
他们真正主宰了美貌与气质的存在，
其他人不过是把美艳的红抹尽两腮。
夏日的花总把夏的风情甜蜜地摆拍，
哪怕它的一生不过是从盛开到默败，
但是一旦它的根染上了卑鄙的尘埃，
卑微的野草也能踩踏它尊严的底牌；
一念之差，再甜的味蕾也只是酸苦难耐；
一朝腐烂，再美的百合姿态比草还破败。

但愿我是 你的夏日

Alack, what poverty my Muse brings forth,
That, having such a scope to show her pride,
The argument all bare is of more worth
Than when it hath my added praise beside.
O blame me not if I no more can write!
Look in your glass, and there appears a face
That over-goes my blunt invention quite,
Dulling my lines, and doing me disgrace.
Were it not sinful, then, striving to mend,
To mar the subject that before was well?
For to no other pass my verses tend
Than of your graces and your gifts to tell;
And more, much more, than in my verse can sit
Your own glass shows you, when you look in it.

Sonnet 103
第 103 首　十四行诗

我的诗神寄来的为何是如此干枯的信件，
明明你一个回眸就已然写尽了风度翩翩，
你的素颜清新无妆点却沉睡了我的笔尖
再甜的赞美词却也说不清我对你的爱恋。
请不要挂念如果某天我迷失在美的语言！
你只需要走到镜前魔镜便会把最美呈现
这迷人的侧脸远胜了我诗里最美的春天，
每一段华丽的字里行间都让我丢尽颜面。
也许你早已发现我的诗里藏满我的狡辩，
再柔美的描写也画不出与你遇见的从前？
我泼墨的落笔只有写到你才会清晰可见
满天飘落的风雪红颜吹散了多久的思念；
千百次想用最美的词描绘你的秀发如烟
镜中的你早已是人间词话里最美的诗篇。

但愿我是　你的夏日

Let not my love be called idolatry,

Nor my beloved as an idol show,

Since all alike my songs and praises be

To one, of one, still such, and ever so.

Kind is my love to-day, to-morrow kind,

Still constant in a wondrous excellence;

Therefore my verse to constancy confin'd,

One thing expressing, leaves out difference.

Fair, kind, and true, is all my argument,

Fair, kind, and true, varying to other words;

And in this change is my invention spent,

Three themes in one, which wondrous scope affords.

Fair, kind, and true, have often liv'd alone,

Which three, till now, never kept seat in one.

Sonnet 105

第 105 首　十四行诗

吾爱不是你口中崇拜的模样，

也不是你眼里那灯光下的偶像，

尽管我所有的歌与赞美辞章

都给了吾爱和永恒的一曲情长。

吾爱把今日的情真写进明日的善良，

绰约的美德是永恒之花在心底绽放；

所以我把韵文也只给坚贞不渝奉上，

这便可摆脱干扰只把唯一的心吟唱。

真善美是我全部爱的所思所想，

真善美是万千咏叹的荡气回肠；

我把他们全部都锁进我诗咏的魔方，

三心归一的奇幻里竟是吾爱的模样。

真善美，叹离殇，子夜未央，天涯各一方，

今宵聚首心灯旁，路漫长，信步不彷徨。

Let me not to the marriage of true minds

Admit impediments; love is not love

Which alters when it alteration finds,

Or bends with the remover to remove.

O no, it is an ever-fixed mark,

That looks on tempests and is never shaken;

It is the star to every wand'ring bark,

Whose worth's unknown, although his height be taken.

Love's not Time's fool, though rosy lips and cheeks

Within his bending sickle's compass come;

Love alters not with his brief hours and weeks,

But bears it out even to the edge of doom.

If this be error and upon me proved,

I never writ, nor no man ever loved.

Sonnet 116

第116首 十四行诗

我还是要用心说,两颗真心的本我

无人能压抑花朵,爱也许会被迷惑

若他改变了轮舵,爱就立即转向左,

若他转念要退缩,爱也立刻去挣脱。

这些绝对是心魔,爱是永恒的灯火,

她面对骤雨瓢泼,也从不委屈让座;

她是星月在闪烁,照亮归途的轮廓,

她高度总有脉络,价值更无法反驳。

爱不受时光弄拨,尽管红颜很洒脱

到头来也逃不过,时光诡计的龌龊;

爱决不会因岁月蹉跎,而改变真我,

即使被末日之神冷漠,也永不漂泊。

假如你们说我错了,或者说,真相与我相左,

那就当我从没写过,我想说,世间无人爱过。

Thy gift, thy tables, are within my brain
Full charactered with lasting memory,
Which shall above that idle rank remain
Beyond all date, even to eternity;
Or at the least, so long as brain and heart
Have faculty by nature to subsist;
Till each to razed oblivion yield his part
Of thee, thy record never can be missed.
That poor retention could not so much hold,
Nor need I tallies thy dear love to score;
Therefore to give them from me was I bold,
To trust those tables that receive thee more;
To keep an adjunct to remember thee
Were to import forgetfulness in me.

Sonnet 122
第 122 首 十四行诗

你赠予我的手册,都已在我脑海里封存
我记得所有韵文和每处文笔的情深意真,
这一切远胜手册里那些无用的文字本身
它将跨越所有时辰,最后终将抵达永恒;
或者至少当我们的大脑和心还彼此共振
至少还能一起体验人间这段有限的生存;
只要大脑和心没有迷失在那遗忘的孤城
那么你的一切便将永远在心底落地生根。
那个单薄的手册无法容纳所有爱的深沉,
我也不必把每一页爱的记录都累计打分;
所以我斗胆把它留给了呼啸而过的东风,
却用更好的方式把你写进人间最美的梦;
人们总一往情深,天真地认为永生才是爱的纯真
而我的爱里只有诚恳,你在我心里,盛开了永恒。

Th'expense of spirit in a waste of shame

Is lust in action; and till action, lust

Is perjured, murd'rous, bloody, full of blame,

Savage, extreme, rude, cruel, not to trust;

Enjoyed no sooner but despised straight;

Past reason hunted, and no sooner had,

Past reason hated as a swallowed bait

On purpose laid to make the taker mad;

Mad in pursuit, and in possession so,

Had, having, and in quest to have, extreme;

A bliss in proof, and proved, a very woe;

Before, a joy proposed; behind, a dream.

All this the world well knows, yet none knows well

To shun the heaven that leads men to this hell.

Sonnet 129

第 129 首　十四行诗

灵魂在耻辱的虚空里被殆尽消亡
是因为情欲在行动里格外地嚣张
伪装阴谋罪恶和责难在精心酝酿，
凶残粗莽和极端便也悄悄地滋长；
于是欢乐也被熬入了卑鄙的毒汤；
为何要露出那样如此渴望的面庞，
可一到手又变成了那厌恶的模样
诱饵仿佛拥有魔力总让人们抓狂；
追求满是疯狂，占有还进而加强，
已有现有和未有里统统满是欲望；
感受中的幸福其实是痛苦的假象；
事前满心欢喜可事后却如梦一场。
人们全以为看到了天堂，其实是在为地狱说谎
不去想，没话讲，去他的权力欲望。

O from what power hast thou this powerful might,

With insufficiency my heart to sway,

To make me give the lie to my true sight,

And swear that brightness doth not grace the day?

Whence hast thou this becoming of things ill,

That in the very refuse of thy deeds

There is such strength and warrantise of skill

That in my mind thy worst all best exceeds?

Who taught thee how to make me love thee more,

The more I hear and see just cause of hate?

O, though I love what others do abhor,

With others thou shouldst not abhor my state:

If thy unworthiness raised love in me,

More worthy I to be beloved of thee.

Sonnet 150

第 150 首 十四行诗

不知你从什么能量中把如此的力量得来，
虽然有瑕疵但是依然能把我的心灵主宰，
对真实所见我谎言否认一定是你在使坏，
断言阳光不会让白日明媚我竟给予喝彩？
是何原因你竟为丑恶换上了美丽的外在，
让你这些无比不堪的种种恶行渐渐释怀
无比的智慧和如此的魅力都在为你站台
让我心中你所有的缺陷远胜了我的青睐？
是谁教会了你如何偷走我心里全部的爱，
尽管所见所闻都在滋长我的反感和愤慨？
虽然我爱的人也非别人欣然接受的姿态，
但你也不该与他人一同来厌烦我的偏爱：
你不是梦里的爱琴海，我的心为何还在澎湃，
我依然会在那里等待，你披着月光向我走来。

John Keats

约翰·济慈
1795—1821

英国浪漫主义诗人,代表作有《致拜伦》《秋颂》《夜莺颂》等。济慈的诗文将现实和浪漫相融合,构成了其独特的诗文风格。

真与美是济慈毕生的精神追求,他曾经在诗中写道:"Beauty is truth, truth is beauty."(美即真,真即美)。济慈在诗中建构了一个真实与美好的世界,使他能够以乐观的态度面对艰难的现实。

济慈出身贫寒,父母早亡,但他天资聪颖,十四五岁就开始学医,后虽然取得医生资格,但是他受到拜伦和雪莱等诗人的影响,决心专门从事诗文创作,选择了弃医从文、创作诗歌的人生道路。

John Keats
约翰 · 济慈

When I Have Fears

Bright Star

To Byron

On Leaving Some Friends at an Early Hour

To Leigh Hunt, Esq.

On the Sea

To—

Sonnet to Spenser

每当我害怕	222
璀璨的繁星	224
致拜伦	226
清晨送别友人	228
致李·亨特先生	230
海浪之上	232
致——	236
致斯宾塞	238

John Keats
约翰·济慈

The Human Seasons

Why Did I Laugh Tonight? No Voice Will Tell

On Death

To Emma

Faery Song

Daisy's Song

O Solitude! If I Must with Thee Dwell

To Autumn

人的季节	240
今夜墨雨无声，我又为何谈笑风生	242
生死无常 皆是虚妄	244
致埃玛	246
仙子的歌	250
雏菊的歌	252
孤独，如果我必须与你同住	254
秋颂	256

When I Have Fears

When I have fears that I may cease to be
Before my pen has gleaned my teeming brain,
Before high piled books, in charactery,
Hold like rich garners the full-ripened grain;
When I behold, upon the night's starred face,
Huge cloudy symbols of a high romance,
And think that I may never live to trace
Their shadows, with the magic hand of chance;
And when I feel, fair creature of an hour!
That I shall never look upon thee more,
Never have relish in the faery power
Of unreflecting love; —then on the shore
Of the wide world I stand alone, and think
Till Love and Fame to nothingness do sink.

每当我害怕

每当我害怕生命就这样画上休止符
我潮水般的思绪在笔尖也无法留住,
好像万卷缤纷的文笔在落幕前倾吐,
如同那饱满的稻谷舞动着心的仓库;
每当我仰望着繁星轻轻地拉开序幕,
凝望最美的浪漫绣成最晴朗的云雾,
然而我怕迷失在那生命尽头的归途
更怕刻意的运笔可能全是画蛇添足;
每当我感慨下一秒时光华丽的脚步!
也许与你的相望永远沉没在忘情湖,
多少次强忍与你这本沉思录的情毒
记录的是夜夜夜夜让爱在心间留宿
天地间岁月的漫步沉思着一世虚无
爱与名的荒芜尘封了我这百年孤独。

Bright Star

璀璨的繁星

Bright star, would I were stedfast as thou art—

Not in lone splendour hung aloft the night

And watching, with eternal lids apart,

Like nature's patient, sleepless Eremite,

The moving waters at their priestlike task

Of pure ablution round earth's human shores,

Or gazing on the new soft-fallen mask

Of snow upon the mountains and the moors—

No—yet still stedfast, still unchangeable,

Pillow'd upon my fair love's ripening breast,

To feel for ever its soft fall and swell,

To feel for ever in a sweet unrest,

Still, still to hear her tender-taken breath,

And so live ever—or else swoon to death.

但愿我能如你般坚定不变——

就像你独悬在天边闪烁着黑夜里最难舍的梦魇

凝望是永恒睁开的双眼留下的感言，

像那情定桃花源的隐士口中的彻夜不眠，

那东流而去的海浪是神父祷告的庄严十诫

像圣水般洗礼着我们一同走过的每一个岸边，

或者凝视着那轻盈又冰清玉洁的白雪

那么温柔地依偎在冷峻的山巅和地老天荒的原野——

可不是吗，我只愿依然坚定不变，

把头藏进她柔软又满是温存的胸脯间，

感受随着心跳徐徐降落又缓缓升起的每寸体贴，

梦醒来岁月在我心里锁进了这首没有风的诗篇，

你宁静淡雅的呼吸轻轻地吻过我窗外的沧海桑田，

永生花盛开的星月夜是否依然能与此诗拥你入眠。

但愿我是　你的夏日

To Byron

Byron! how sweetly sad thy melody!
Attuning still the soul to tenderness,
As if soft Pity, with unusual stress,
Had touch'd her plaintive lute, and thou, being by,
Hadst caught the tones, nor suffer'd them to die.
O'ershadowing sorrow doth not make thee less
Delightful: thou thy griefs dost dress
With a bright halo, shining beamily,
As when a cloud a golden moon doth veil,
Its sides are ting'd with a resplendent glow,
Through the dark robe oft amber rays prevail,
And like fair veins in sable marble flow;
Still warble, dying swan! still tell the tale,
The enchanting tale, the tale of pleasing woe.

致拜伦

拜伦!你独有的音律里满是甜蜜的伤痕!
那恰到好处的和弦让柔情和心灵在共振,
好像温和的遗憾携带着不同寻常的深沉,
指尖流淌着忧郁的琴声,你纯真的灵魂,
记下了全部的音程,这旋律便得以永恒。
阴沉的忧伤也丝毫没有把你的愉悦封存
我听见旋律背后你暗藏的所有风雨兼程
带着明亮的光轮,照进人间每一抹黄昏,
好似一朵云彩轻轻遮掩了金黄色的月痕,
在月的边缘镶嵌着无比灿烂的浮生若梦,
琥珀色的光终于冲破了黑色长袍的围困,
看起来像貂纹大理石上流淌的华丽纹身;
快临别的天鹅,依旧在吟唱着那个古老而又动人的传闻,
文笔如此传神,是你用芳醇亲吻了人间所有悲伤的离分。

Give me a golden pen, and let me lean

On heaped-up flowers, in regions clear, and far;

Bring me a tablet whiter than a star,

Or hand of hymning angel, when 'tis seen

The silver strings of heavenly harp atween:

And let there glide by many a pearly car,

Pink robes, and wavy hair, and diamond jar,

And half-discovered wings, and glances keen.

The while let music wander round my ears,

And as it reaches each delicious ending,

Let me write down a line of glorious tone,

And full of many wonders of the spheres:

For what a height my spirit is contending!

'Tis not content so soon to be alone.

On Leaving Some Friends at an Early Hour
清晨送别友人

能否给我一支金色的笔来描写永恒
在空灵的远方我依偎着那鲜花蔓藤；
能否给我带来一份白过星辰的纸本，
或是一双天使的手满是颂歌的虔诚
在竖琴的银弦上舞动那神圣的乐声：
挂满珍珠的彩车在欢呼雀跃里奔腾，
那粉衣裳那飞扬的头发和钻石玉盆，
还有半露的翅膀和期盼的眼波深深。
就让这天籁之音在我耳边相伴一生，
当乐章终于接近了华丽美好的尾声，
请让我写下这行高贵典雅的抒情文，
诗句里满是那星空之上的美梦成真：
我的灵魂穷其一生只为攀登那更高耸的山峰！
它不愿在时光里孤独静等，余生便不再沉沦。

To Leigh Hunt, Esq.

Glory and loveliness have passed away;
For if we wander out in early morn,
No wreathed incense do we see upborne
Into the east, to meet the smiling day;
No crowd of nymphs soft voic'd and young, and gay,
In woven baskets bringing ears of corn,
Roses, and pinks, and violets, to adorn
The shrine of Flora in her early May.
But there are left delights as high as these,
And I shall ever bless my destiny,
That in a time, when under pleasant trees
Pan is no longer sought, I feel a free,
A leafy luxury, seeing I could please
With these poor offerings a man like thee.

致李·亨特先生

那些光辉和柔情都早已消逝在那一江春水；
犹记当年我们在黎明漫步沐浴着一缕朝晖，
我们没有欣赏到那袅袅的炊烟纷飞了赞美
它早已飞向东方为迎接微笑的白昼在准备；
没有发现甜美可爱的年轻仙女们成群结队，
手里挽着的编织篮里满是沉甸甸的玉米穗，
用玫瑰花、石竹花和紫罗兰一起加以点缀
在早春五月即将到来的万花神的圣地丰碑。
但我们依然有诗歌让欢乐与我们形影相随，
所以我将永远感激今生被赐予了如此恩惠，
在某个时期，我在林间宜人的树荫下沉睡
虽然再也没有机会品味牧神潘午后的甜美，
可我依然能在绿荫里感受人间所有惬意的明媚
那我希望这首贫乏的献礼能伴你今生一世无悔。

但愿我是　你的夏日

On the Sea

It keeps eternal whisperings around
Desolate shores, and with its mighty swell
Gluts twice ten thousand Caverns, till the spe[ll]
Of Hecate leaves them their old shadowy sou[nd]
Often 'tis in such gentle temper found,
That scarcely will the very smallest shell
Be moved for days from where it sometime fe[ll]
When last the winds of Heaven were unbound[.]
Oh, ye! who have your eye-balls vexed and ti[red]
Feast them upon the wideness of the sea;
Oh ye! whose ears are dinned with uproar rud[e]
Or fed too much with cloying melody—
Sit ye near some old cavern's mouth and broo[d]
Until ye start, as if the sea-nymphs quired!

大海滔滔不绝地把永恒的絮语诉说
满是荒芜的海岸边翻滚着层层旋涡
汹涌的海浪顷刻间把千万岩洞淹没
直到神用咒语唤回往日的幽深静默。
大海也时常把温柔和宁静埋进心窝,
然后你会发现那微小的贝壳在角落
好几天它也没有被谁给轻轻地挪过,
一如当初狂风把它卷来时一样落魄。
如果你的双眼被迷惑也被疲倦污浊,
那就放眼于这大海壮丽的浩瀚广阔;
如果你无法忍受喧哗声折磨着耳膜,
或是这些甜腻的旋律你已听了太多——
那就试着去海边的岩洞口静坐冥想,时光斑驳
直到心里恍然听见海上仙女吟唱的,岁月蹉跎!

海浪

之上

To—

Time's sea hath been five years at its slow ebb;

Long hours have to and fro let creep the sand,

Since I was tangled in thy beauty's web,

And snared by the ungloving of thy hand.

And yet I never look on midnight sky,

But I behold thine eyes' well-memoried light;

I cannot look upon the rose's dye,

But to thy cheek my soul doth take its flight:

I cannot look on any budding flower,

But my fond ear, in fancy at thy lips,

And hearkening for a love-sound, doth devour

Its sweets in the wrong sense. —Thou dost eclipse

Every delight with sweet remembering,

And grief unto my darling joys dost bring.

致——

时间的大海在潮起潮落里已经走了五年岁月；
漫长的时间匍匐在流沙之间反复上演着离别，
自从我坠入你美丽容颜编织的网中无尽长夜，
褪去手套的纤纤玉手竟会让我此生相思欲绝。
然而每当我仰望午夜的星空里月光如此浓烈，
照进我的思念让我沉醉你目光里的温柔体贴；
我无法再正视嫣红的玫瑰哪怕染色逐渐凋谢，
但我深情的灵魂好似已飞到你脸旁如此迅捷：
我无法再正视盛开的花朵哪怕仅是余光一瞥，
我多情的耳朵仿佛就靠在你唇边无比的真切，
你那爱的声线如此皎洁是我今生唯一的独缺
在幻想的甘甜里渐渐迷失直到我沉浸这错觉
甜蜜的回忆斑驳了今生的喜悦，晓风残月，情字难写，
心底的欢乐被惆怅锁进了冬夜，故情未歇，寂寞如雪。

Spenser! A jealous honourer of thine,

A forester deep in thy midmost trees,

Did last eve ask my promise to refine

Some English that might strive thine ear to please.

But Elfin Poet, 'tis impossible

For an inhabitant of wintry earth

To rise like Phoebus with a golden quill

Fire-wing'd and make a morning in his mirth.

It is impossible to escape from toil

O' the sudden and receive thy spiriting:

The flower must drink the nature of the soil

Before it can put forth its blossoming:

Be with me in the summer days, and I

Will for thine honour and his pleasure try.

Sonnet to Spenser
致斯宾塞

斯宾塞！有一个嫉妒你的崇拜者你是否知道，
他就隐居在你小径通幽的树林里某一处芳草，
昨夜他要求我承诺再次拿出我最珍贵的羽毛
精心构思创作出能在你耳边萦绕的那曲离骚。
然而，我伟大的诗神啊，我要如何才能做到
对一个长期居住在冬日里的我要怎样去思考
我不能像太阳神那样给予火焰般金色的拥抱
然后以他金灿灿的羽毛为笔勾勒清晨的欢笑。
他也绝不可能立刻便逃离出被困已久的苦劳
接着突然间也完全吸收了你精神的灵丹妙药：
花儿只有饮下足够的土壤里无比纯然的养料
才能在盛开的季节绽放得绚丽多娇分外妖娆：
如果凑巧，阳光正好，我们是否可以在这个夏季把彼此找到
为致敬你的荣耀，成全他的美好，我又拾起了最珍贵的羽毛。

Four Seasons fill the measure of the year;
There are four seasons in the mind of man:
He has his lusty Spring, when fancy clear
Takes in all beauty with an easy span:
He has his Summer, when luxuriously
Spring's honied cud of youthful thought he loves
To ruminate, and by such dreaming high
Is nearest unto heaven: quiet coves
His soul has in its Autumn, when his wings
He furleth close; contented so to look
On mists in idleness—to let fair things
Pass by unheeded as a threshold brook.
He has his Winter too of pale misfeature,
Or else he would forego his mortal nature.

人的季节
The Human Seasons

春夏秋冬的如约而至等候了人间一年；
人们的心灵深处也有四季交替的感言：
他有生机盎然的春天，满是柔绿如烟
幻想仅一眼便能把所有天下至美看遍；
转眼他便走入了夏天，漫天飞红片剪
晓春岁月的爱恋回味起来是那般香甜
沉浸在这甜蜜的思念，梦醒依旧庭院
天际翱翔的梦想带他飞向那天上人间
他的灵魂宁静在湾边，黄叶静数秋天
他收拢了疲倦的羽翼遥望从前山色远
往事如烟自在地想念，锦瑟花间柔闲
恍若门前溪水渐渐飘远你却花丛冷眼。
他终将在终点拥抱姗姗来迟的冬天，苍白了岁月的容颜，
不然他便是超越了人间生死的极限，来世再把今生成全。

但愿我是 你的夏日

Why Did I Laugh Tonight? No Voice Will Tell

Why did I laugh tonight? No voice will tell;
No god, no demon of severe response,
Deigns to reply from heaven or from hell.
Then to my human heart I turn at once—
Heart! thou and I are here, sad and alone;
Say, wherefore did I laugh? O mortal pain!
O darkness! darkness! ever must I moan,
To question heaven and hell and heart in vain!
Why did I laugh? I know this being's lease—
My fancy to it's utmost blisses spreads:
Yet would I on this very midnight cease,
And all the world's gaudy ensigns see in shreds.
Verse, fame and beauty are intense indeed
But death intenser—death is life's high meed.

今夜墨雨无声，我又为何谈笑风生

我为何谈笑风生，寂静在午夜生根，依然无从听闻：
上帝没有出声，也没有听见恶魔那冷酷无比的口吻，
也许不论天堂或是地狱，都不愿为给我回应而屈尊。
于是我作罢，即刻转向我这颗凡人的心灵扪心自问——
心灵啊！我们相伴今生，却一度伤神直至孑然一身；
那为何我依然谈笑风生？唉，我这痛苦不堪的伤痕！
唉，黑暗，黑暗的时辰，我今生何时才能停止怨恨，
向天堂询问，向地狱追问，向心灵质问，浮生若梦！
为何我依然谈笑风生？我知道人间的租期仅此一生——
我让幻想向远方延伸，伸展到那极乐之地远离红尘；
也许今晚午夜的时辰，我便要告别人间所有的爱恨，
世间的彩旗碎落纷纷，在我眼里都封存在永夜的梦。
诗歌韵文，一世名声，绝世佳人，我承认，都是人间最动情的芳芬，
但死亡更香醇，生命最诚挚的感恩，因为只有它能把转瞬写进永恒。

Can death be sleep, when life is but a dream,

And scenes of bliss pass as a phantom by?

The transient pleasures as a vision seem,

And yet we think the greatest pain's to die.

How strange it is that man on earth should roam,

And lead a life of woe, but not forsake

His rugged path; nor dare he view alone

His future doom which is but to awake.

死亡或许是长眠一场，倘若生命只是梦里时光，
然后那些幸福的模样，为何如幻影般转瞬消亡？
那些片刻的愉悦欢畅，过眼云烟般匆忙地离场，
然而我们固执的妄想，认定死亡是最痛的悲伤。

这是多么奇怪的景象，人活世上却注定要流浪，
忍耐今生所有的凄凉，他仍然怀着固执的念想
走向远方无尽的迷茫，亦不敢试着去看清真相
他殊不知所谓的死亡，不过是永远告别了梦乡。

On Death

生死无常　皆是虚妄

O come, dearest Emma! the rose is full blown,
And the riches of Flora are lavishly strown;
The air is all softness, and chrystal the streams,
And the west is resplendently clothed in beams.

We will hasten, my fair, to the opening glades,
The quaintly carv'd seats, and the freshening shades;
Where the fairies are chanting their evening hymns,
And in the last sun-beam the sylph lightly swims.

And when thou art weary, I'll find thee a bed,
Of mosses, and flowers, to pillow thy head;
There, beauteous Emma, I'll sit at thy feet,
While my story of love I enraptur'd repeat.

亲爱的埃玛,是否,你看见了玫瑰花绽放的温柔,
然后花神便慷慨地给大地撒满了珍宝,何等富有;
空气里满是一份轻柔,溪水看起来如水晶般剔透,
西边天际披着华丽的丝绸沐浴着霞光向往着不朽。

要务必加快我们的行走,去寻找林中广阔的绿洲,
那雕刻精美的石凳和林中绿荫的倒影会为你停留;
那儿有仙女咏唱着黄昏的赞美诗渐渐地夜落山丘,
在夕阳的余晖里小精灵们向着光明处轻盈地畅游。

每当你感到疲倦的时候,我为你寻找温暖的床头,
而你便可以枕靠在青苔和鲜花的枕头上梦落三秋;
至美的埃玛我是否能端坐在你脚边看清你的眼眸,
然后把故事里的爱恨情仇全为你细说,毫无保留。

To
Emma
致埃玛

但愿我是 你的夏日

So fondly I'll breathe, and so softly I'll sigh,

Thou wilt think that some amorous zephyr is nigh;

Ah! no—as I breathe it, I press thy fair knee,

And then, thou wilt know that the sigh comes from me.

Then why, lovely girl, should we lose all these blisses?

That mortal's a fool who such happiness misses;

So smile acquiescence, and give me thy hand,

With love-looking eyes, and with voice sweetly bland.

深情的呼吸是我的挽留，轻轻的哀叹是我在消愁，
你竟以为是来自远方多情的微风相守在你的左右；
知否，知否，我的呼吸正向着你的双膝缓缓漫游，
等到那时候，你定会察觉这叹息里满是我的等候。

我亲爱的红颜翠袖，难道我们要让幸福统统溜走？
凡人时常会愚钝腐朽，竟错过了如此欢愉的邂逅；
你是否愿意让我今生执子之手，多想看见你在微笑着对我点头，
目光里爱意情柔，嗓音满是甜蜜清秀，今生无缘，来世有缘否。

Shed no tear! oh, shed no tear!

The flower will bloom another year;

Weep no more—oh, weep no more!

Young buds sleep in the root's white core.

Dry your eyes—oh, dry your eyes!

For I was taught in Paradise

To ease my breast of melodies—

Shed no tear.

Faery Song 仙子的歌

Overhead! look overhead!

'Mong the blossoms white and red—

Look up, look up' I flutter now

On this fresh pomegranate bough.

See me! 'tis this silvery bill

Ever cures the good man's ill.

Shed no tear! oh, shed no tear!

The flower will bloom another year.

Adieu, adieu—I fly, adieu!

I vanish in the heaven's blue—

Adieu, adieu!

请不要留下眼泪！千万别留下眼泪！
花儿明年依然会重现最艳丽的花蕾；
所以不要再流泪，不要再流下泪水！
稚嫩的花苞在根茎洁白的心底沉睡。
请擦干你的泪水！擦干残留的眼泪！
沐浴天堂的光辉我领悟了这份恩惠
如何写意地发挥这满腔旋律的柔美——
便是，请不要留下眼泪。

头顶天空的深邃！看看头顶的深邃！
穿过前方那红白相间的鲜花的聚会——
抬头让目光跟随，是谁让空气沉醉
是我在茂盛的石榴树枝上振翅待飞。
瞧见我没，就是风中那银色的优美
能永远把好人治愈不会被疾病摧毁。
请不要留下眼泪！千万别留下眼泪！
花儿明年依然会重现最艳丽的花蕾。
再会了，再会，我即将起飞，再会！
我会在纯蓝的天边消失进爱的无悔——
再会！我去去就回！

Daisy's Song

The sun, with his great eye,

Sees not so much as I;

And the moon, all silver-proud,

Might as well be in a cloud.

And O the spring, the spring!

I lead the life of a king!

Couch'd in the teeming grass,

I spy each pretty lass.

I look where no one dares,

And I stare where no one stares,

And when the night is nigh,

Lambs bleat my lullaby.

雏菊的歌

太阳是永恒的，像巨大的眼睛高悬着，
可为何，视野却没有我看到的更广呢；
月亮也永恒的，银辉是她骄傲的颜色，
也忐忑，时常被乌云遮挡了她的亮泽。

谁来了，是春天么，是的！春天来了！
我精心地把生活建设，国王般的快乐！
然后惬意地躺卧着，草木苍翠的天河，
无意瞥见了，每个少女都是倾城的歌。

那些无人敢去看的，我全部都在看着，
那些无人去凝望的，我全部都凝望着，
然后当夜幕降临的时刻，人间变暗了，
羊羔为我唱着催眠的歌，愿我都记得。

O Solitude!
If I Must with Thee Dwell

O Solitude! if I must with thee dwell,

Let it not be among the jumbled heap

Of murky buildings; climb with me the steep,—

Nature's observatory—whence the dell,

In flowery slopes, its river's crystal swell,

May seem a span; let me thy vigils keep

'Mongst boughs pavilion'd, where the deer's swift leap

Startles the wild bee from the fox-glove bell.

But though I'll gladly trace these scenes with thee,

Yet the sweet converse of an innocent mind,

Whose words are images of thoughts refin'd,

Is my soul's pleasure; and it sure must be

Almost the highest bliss of human-kind,

When to thy haunts two kindred spirits flee.

孤独，如果我必须与你今生同住某个居巢，
我希望不是那层层堆砌的大楼，阴暗寂寥
我想邀请你与我一同相伴今朝，攀岩登高，——
然后在最高处把自然极目远眺，幽谷凌霄，
坡上的芳草分外妖娆，河流像水晶在闪耀，
仿佛仅一步之遥，那就让我把你紧紧依靠
在那茂盛的绿荫怀抱，小鹿正欢快地舞蹈
稍许惊吓野蜜蜂便迅速飞离毛地黄的花苞。
尽管我将欣然与你今生相伴踏遍天涯海角，
却更渴望与纯净的心灵促膝长谈时的美好，
她的谈吐写意地勾勒着每一缕思绪的美貌，
我听见灵魂欢快的心跳，想必我已经找到
这人间幸福至美的欢笑，它的味道，甜得刚好，美妙，
是两颗真心在向你奔跑，无人知晓，没人打扰，真好。

孤独，
如果我必须与你同住

但愿我是 你的夏日

To Autumn
秋　　颂

Season of mists and mellow fruitfulness,
Close bosom-friend of the maturing sun,
Conspiring with him how to load and bless
With fruit the vines that round the thatch-eaves run;
To bend with apples the mossed cottage-trees,
And fill all fruit with ripeness to the core;
To swell the gourd, and plump the hazel shells
With a sweet kernel; to set budding more,
And still more, later flowers for the bees,
Until they think warm days will never cease,
For Summer has o'er-brimmed their clammy cell.

缤纷的果实把四季的雾霭酿进了这壶醉人的秋，
在那夜曲的最后用成熟的阳光写下了执子之手，
茅草青青的屋檐下藤蔓还在等待那安静的邂逅
期待她用满天硕硕的果实揭开酝酿已久的密谋；
你猜那是谁在淘气地摇晃轩窗外苹果树的枝头，
又是谁把果实裹上了温柔也把心底濡濡地熟透；
岁月从壮硕的葫芦旁溜走隐匿在榛子壳的左右
用甜蜜悄悄地在每个果核心底种下了爱的轻柔，
不辞辛劳的蜜蜂正把铺满大地的花朵尽兴地收，
那久远的时光把温暖刻进了每一日梦境的背后，
仲夏夜那湿漉漉的鸟巢依旧在吟唱着为你停留。

但愿我是 你的夏日

Who hath not seen thee oft amid thy store?

Sometimes whoever seeks abroad may find

Thee sitting careless on a granary floor,

Thy hair soft-lifted by the winnowing wind;

Or on a half-reaped furrow sound asleep,

Drowsed with the fume of poppies, while thy hook

Spares the next swath and all its twined flowers;

And sometimes like a gleaner thou dost keep

Steady thy laden head across a brook;

Or by a cyder-press, with patient look,

Thou watchest the last oozings hours by hours.

又到了可以在繁忙忙的仓廪与你捉迷藏的时候？
最后在漫天花雨的田野找到了你那清澈的眼眸
就那样慵懒地随意地欢喜地坐在打谷场的尽头，
明媚悠扬的风深情地在秀美的发间吻下了不朽；
你沉沉地把劳作过半的犁沟拖进梦的月满西楼，
虞美人花语带幽香在你的身旁诉说着一叶深秋
好让满是汗水的镰刀也在花丛攒簇旁片刻午休；
有时候你又好似拾穗人沿着田间溪河静静地走
载满一袋袋沉甸甸的收获越过岁月的细水长流；
你是那么专注地凝望着果实缓缓地被榨汁入酒，
生怕最美的陈酿在时光的魔术里不经意被偷走。

但愿我是 你的夏日

Where are the songs of Spring? Ay, where are they?

Think not of them, thou hast thy music too—

While barred clouds bloom the soft-dying day,

And touch the stubble-plains with rosy hue;

Then in a wailful choir the small gnats mourn

Among the river sallows, borne aloft

Or sinking as the light wind lives or dies;

And full-grown lambs loud bleat from hilly bourn;

Hedge-crickets sing; and now with treble soft

The redbreast whistles from a garden-croft;

And gathering swallows twitter in the skies.

那春天的百花之歌是否被沙鸥藏进了山涧碧柳？
无碍秋月谱写的夜神之曲一样如你般眉清目秀——
你看那黯淡的云还在夜幕到来之前激情地挥手，
把爱的玫瑰胭脂红染进了原野量身定制的丝绸；
序曲略带哀伤的鼓点像轻盈的小飞虫们在疾走
又像河柳随风把沿途的风景向上向上慢慢地修
而下落瞬间微岚却淡去了生命全部的爱恨情仇；
那高扬的节奏是山谷的群羊们成长的高亢之吼；
和弦的律动是篱下蟋蟀们高声演绎的生命之柔
红胸知更鸟那独奏的口哨带来的是多久的等候；
落幕前云燕那高声一叹成全了你我的这曲清秋。

特此鸣谢协同创作者：

洪苏昕　洪乐维　忻然　李翕然　罗亚明　江城子

上海水问教育科技有限公司